SACRIFICED
and
Reclaimed

THE SOLDIER'S DARING WIDOW

BY
BREE WOLF

This is a work of fiction. Names, characters, businesses, places, brands, media, events and incidents are either the products of the author's imagination or used in a fictitious manner.

Any resemblance to actual persons, living or dead, or actual events is purely coincidental.

Cover Art by Victoria Cooper
Copyright © 2018 Bree Wolf

Papaerback ISBN: 978-1980805441
Hardcover ISBN: 978-3-96482-113-3

www.breewolf.com

All Rights Reserved

This book or any portion thereof may not be reproduced or used in any manner whatsoever without the express written permission of the author except for the use of brief quotations in a book review.

To my Devoted Readers
Christa Cox-Watanabe
Debbie Clatterbuck
Melissa Joy Herrin
Pamela Dobbins
Ruth Ann Campbell
May You Never Leave Me

Acknowledgments

Publishing a book is a team effort, unparalleled in this world. So many people invest their time and heart into this project to see it listed. My thank-you to all of you who've helped with feedback, typo detection, character and plot development, editing, formatting, cover creation, and the biggie...spreading the word...so that countless readers can now enjoy these stories of love's second chance.

I owe you all so much!

Thank you!

SACRIFICED *and* Reclaimed

Prologue

England, Autumn 1805 (or a variation thereof)

As she climbed the small slope north of the village she had grown up in, Meagan Dunning felt as though each agonising step took her further away from the life she had loved. Dragging her feet, she forced herself onward until she reached the top, a small mount, which overlooked the tiny village.

Gazing down at the handful of homes clustered around a market square, Meagan could not help but remember the many times she had come up here with her husband. How often had they stood like this, in this very spot, and gazed down at the sleepy village? How often had they spoken of a future spent away from here, out in the world? How often had she looked at him and believed that-like her-he was merely daydreaming?

At least, until the day he had enlisted.

Before Meagan knew what was happening, her husband shipped out, following a call she could not understand. And yet, she had seen the sense of adventure in his eyes that had always been there when they had spoken of a different future. A future different from that of their parents, living and dying in the same small village, never to see anything farther away than a few miles.

Now, her husband was dead.

Closing her eyes, Meagan inhaled a deep breath, willing her tears away. After all, she had already cried a lifetime's worth of tears upon learning the news. Was there any use in weeping day in and day out? Would it do her any good? Did she not have two small children to think of?

Unbidden, a sob tore from Meagan's throat at the thought of her now fatherless children. Never would Matthew ride on his father's shoulders again. Never would little Erin be cooed to sleep by the sound of his voice. Would she even remember him? After all, she had only been a babe.

Wiping a sleeve over her eyes, Meagan refocused her gaze onto the small houses down in the valley, her gaze gliding from one to the other. How often had she spotted her husband walking toward her from up here as she sat in the grass, holding her little daughter, her son playing beside her?

Two years had passed since then.

And yet, it seemed like yesterday.

Her heart still ached whenever she thought of her husband. Tears would sting her eyes, and sobs rose in her throat, and her heart would hurt in a way that she sometimes believed it must surely break in half.

But it did not.

The wound was not fatal. It pained her every day, but she continued, doomed to live the life that had been theirs by herself.

Meagan shook her head. No, that was not true. She was not alone. She had her children, and she could not deny that they brought her much joy. However, no matter what they did -having supper, playing in the fields or whispering to each other at nighttime- she always felt her husband's absence. As though his loss had torn a hole into her life that was simply always there.

Always reminding her of what she had lost.

Of what could have been...if he had stayed.

"Meagan!"

At the sound of his voice, her heart froze, and her inner eye conjured an image of her smiling husband, his eyes aglow with mischief as he chased her through the tall-stemmed grass.

Although her mind knew that it could not be, Meagan had come to realise that her heart had not yet fully accepted the loss of her other half. Often, she found herself waking from dreams that seemed so real that she reached out a hand across the pillow expecting to find her husband beside her. Only when the dream slowly faded away did reality reclaim her, bringing with it excruciating pain that spread through her entire being.

Closing her eyes for but a moment, Meagan took a deep breath before turning to face reality once more. As expected, it was not Edward, not her husband, who came walking toward her, but his best friend Derek McKnight.

And still, her heart ached at having its hopes disappointed once more.

"I've been looking for you," Derek addressed her, his long legs carrying him closer as he watched her through slightly narrowed eyes. Although they had never been close-he had merely been her husband's best friend-she could tell that he was concerned for her, for his best friend's wife.

No, not wife.

Widow.

Meagan swallowed. "I needed...some time to think."

As he came to stand before her, his dark gaze held hers, searching. Then he nodded. "I understand," was all he said, and from the look in his eyes, Meagan knew it to be true.

Derek McKnight, a farmer's son, had always possessed the ability to read those around him. Nothing and no one could hide from his scrutinising gaze, and it had been that sharp-mindedness that had guided him through the war unscathed.

Unlike Edward, Derek had found glory and triumph in his deeds and had even been awarded the title of a baron and given his own estate. Now, he was Lord Ainsworth.

And yet, he was here, staying true to the promise he had made her husband.

To look after her.

When Derek had returned, Meagan had not been able to help herself to gaze past his shoulder, her eyes immediately searching for her husband. They had always been close, and it had seemed natural that Edward would be by Derek's side. Had it not always been thus?

"I need your answer," Derek reminded her, his shoulders tense as he waited.

Meagan knew she ought to accept his offer. And yet, she hesitated.

Once more she turned to the small village at her feet, her eyes seeking out the small home she had shared with her husband. "I don't know if I can," she spoke as a soft breeze brushed over her cheeks, carrying her words into the world. "This place holds all our memories. If I leave it, what do I have left?"

Behind her, Derek drew in a slow breath. "He will never leave you, no matter where you are. His memory is not tied to a place, but to you and your children."

Meagan nodded. "Ye're right, and still, I feel as though I'd betray him by leavin'." She turned to face Derek, fresh tears streaming down her face. "My mind knows that he's dead. But my heart still has hope. What am I to do?"

"Think of your children."

Shifting her gaze, Meagan looked over Derek's shoulder at his mother's kind face. With sure steps, Bessy approached them, Meagan's children, Matthew and Erin, trailing in her wake.

"Mama!" her daughter squealed and threw herself into Meagan's arms.

Hugging her tightly, Meagan smiled at her son, his dark brown eyes so much like his father's.

"Your husband," Bessy began, her kind eyes holding Meagan's, "was very dear to me." Nodding, she smiled, but it was a smile full of sadness and sorrow. "I know that ye don't have any family left here, but I...," she glanced at her son, "we want ye to know that we will always be here for ye and your children. Come with us. We will look after ye if ye let us. I promise that ye and your children will never be alone."

Touched, Meagan sighed, feeling her daughter snuggle into her shoulder as her son came to stand beside her, slipping his little hand into hers. "Thank ye," she whispered before turning her gaze to Derek. "We shall go with ye then."

The corners of his mouth twitched, but he did not say a word. Instead, he turned to Matthew and drew the boy away as his mother stepped forward to take Erin from Meagan's arms.

As she watched them walk down the hill, Meagan once more turned to face the small village. "Goodbye," she whispered as tears streamed down her face. "I shall never forget ye. I promise to carry ye with me wherever I go."

Then she turned and followed the others toward a new life.

A life without her husband.

Chapter One
BROKEN

On the Continent, Autumn 1806

One Year Later

Sitting on a high cliff top overlooking the ocean, Edward Dunning stared at the distant horizon before his gaze once more shifted and he glanced down at the rolling waves as they crashed against the hard rock beneath.

Every morning, he climbed the steep slope to the top, leaning heavily on his cane as he forced his legs to move. Although his right leg did as he wanted, his left leg was more a hindrance than a help.

Injured on the battlefield, Edward had lost consciousness and been left for dead. At least two days had passed before he had awoken, only to find himself in a field surrounded by the bodies of his fallen comrades, the smell of blood and death assaulting his senses.

With his left knee shattered beyond repair, he had dragged himself off the field. His strength had begun to dwindle with the effort it had taken him to not give himself over to despair. At some point, he had passed out again.

When he had opened his eyes once more, he had found himself

inside stone walls, tugged into the comfort of a bed. Gazing around, Edward had taken note of the scarce furnishings, the heavy wooden cross on the wall and the distant sound of ringing bells.

A convent.

Closing his eyes, Edward had sunk back into the pillow, relieved not to have been taken prisoner. Someone had to have found him and taken pity on him, bringing him here.

Thus, had begun his long journey back to health.

Or at least as far as that was possible.

For although the wound on his leg had been cleaned and neatly wrapped in bandages, there had been nothing anyone could have done about his shattered knee. He would never be able to bend it again, doomed to walk with a cane for the rest of his life, moving his stiff leg forward in a half-circle so as not to upend his balance.

As he sat on the cliff top, Edward shifted his gaze down to his left leg as it rested before him, stretched out as though seeking to trip anyone who dared to approach him. For the thousandth time, he shook his head as though in disbelief, unable to make his peace with the past.

And yet, Edward knew that he deserved it.

Even before that fateful day, he had come to realise that his dreams and hopes had been a mere folly. Triumph and glory were not to be found on a battlefield. Only blood and death. There was no life, no adventure. Only horror and loss.

Looking at his leg, Edward knew that he had carelessly thrown away the life he had had, not realising at the time how fortunate he had been.

Now, he knew.

Now, it was too late.

His leg served as a constant reminder of his mistake as well as its consequences.

Once more, Edward glanced over the edge of the cliff top, wondering when the day would come that he would find the courage to end his miserable existence. He knew he ought to. He knew there was nothing left for him. And so, he walked up the steep slope to the top every morning, praying that today would be the day that would end all the pain, all the suffering.

And yet, every night, he found himself walking back down.

Again, Edward closed his eyes, only to see his wife's beautiful face floating before him. "Meagan," he whispered as he reached out a hand to trace the line of her jaw, her blue eyes shining brighter than her golden hair. Never had she seemed more like an angel than she did then and there.

An angel that was out of his reach as his hands grasped at nothing.

Edward sighed. He had had it all.

A beautiful wife, two wonderful children and a comfortable home.

A peaceful life.

And what had he done? He had thrown it all away for the distant notion of adventure, of glory, of…

He could not even say anymore.

All Edward remembered was the desperate desire not to end like his father, like so many of his neighbours, doomed to live an uneventful life, living and dying in the same small village all their lives. He remembered that he did not want to be merely ordinary, one of many, indistinguishable in the crowd. He remembered that back then he could not think of a worse fate than spending his days in his home village.

Now, Edward knew that it had been heaven on earth, for now he knew what hell felt like, and he could not help but wish that he had known then.

Once more, his thoughts turned to his family. More than three years had passed since he had left, since he had last seen them. More than two years had passed since he had been left for dead.

More than once, Edward had tried to picture the moment his wife had been told of his death. He had imagined tears running down her cheeks as she had sunk down, her gaze staring into the distance, unseeing, as disbelief claimed her mind and heart.

Had she mourned him? Of course, she had. After all, they had been in love for the better part of their lives. But for how long?

How had she continued without him? And with two small children no less?

Edward cringed at the thought, and once more guilt rose as he remembered that he had not thought of what would happen if he were not to return from his adventure. How could he have been so selfish? So foolish?

Listening to the waves crash against the rock, Edward wondered for the thousandth time if his wife was even still his wife. Had she remarried? Did their children have a new father now? One who would put their well-being before his own foolish dreams?

Edward knew that after everything he had done, he ought to wish her a happy life with a man who loved her unconditionally by her side.

But he could not as he still thought of her as his, even though he knew she was not. He had given up his claim on her long ago.

Pushing himself off the rock he had been sitting on since that morning, Edward stumbled toward the cliff face, dragging his left leg behind him. His heart thudded in his chest, and he felt the cold wind attack his skin, the promise of winter on its wings. Leaning forward, he gazed down into the churning water, a wet grave.

Inhaling deeply, Edward leaned forward more and more until he reached the point where his balance became unhinged. Instantly, he shrank back, wondering what kept him from ending it all.

Again, his wife's face appeared before his inner eye, and Edward realised that he would never be ready to depart this world without knowing that his family was all right.

Stepping back, he took a deep breath as his resolve strengthened. He would go home. He would see with his own eyes that his family was fine, that they were better off without him. And then he would return to this spot...and hopefully find peace.

Chapter Two
A NEW BEGINNING

England, January 1807

A Few Months Later

Leaning on the cane Derek had fashioned for her, Meagan hobbled through the snow toward the remnants of her cottage. Six-year-old Matthew and 3-year-old Erin ran ahead, throwing snowballs at each other and squealing in delight whenever one of them found its mark. "Don't aim too high," Meagan counselled them, "or ye might lose an eye."

As the children continued to play, Meagan's eyes slid over the caved-in cottage. Only a fortnight ago, a terrible storm had uprooted an old tree by the side of their home, bringing it crashing down onto the cottage's roof. It had collapsed as though made of paper, burying her and Erin inside. Matthew, though, had been able to find a way out and had gone to Huntington House for help.

With her foot stuck under a heavy beam, Meagan had waited in the dark, unable to reach her unconscious daughter across the room. Those moments had been the worst of her life, and even remembering them now brought tears to her eyes.

Glancing over at her children, Meagan found her son standing by the uprooted tree, sadness in his dark brown eyes. When he caught her looking, he stepped closer, his gaze returning to the fallen tree. "It was the perfect tree," he mumbled, sighing with regret. "There is none other like it."

Placing a hand on her son's shoulder, Meagan smiled down at him. "Ye'll find another. Just ye wait. It may not be the same, but it will be a new challenge, a new adventure, and with time, ye'll figure out how to climb it."

Matthew nodded as his little sister came strolling over, her big blue eyes gliding over the fallen tree. "Can I climb, too?"

"Ye're too young," Matthew said with all the wisdom and life experience a six-year-old could muster. "Climbin' trees is dangerous."

Erin frowned. "Why?"

"What happens if ye fall?"

"I won't fall," Erin said, a stern look coming to her eyes as she held her brother's gaze. "I'll hold tight."

Leaving her children to discuss the art of tree climbing, Meagan hobbled back to the collapsed structure, and once again, the night of the storm resurfaced in her mind.

Vividly, she remembered the howling wind and the creaking beams as she had sat waiting in the dark, fear clawing at her heart. It had been a terrifying night, and yet, it had also shown Meagan that she had been wrong to live her life separate from others.

After the loss of her husband, a part of Meagan had reasoned that loss could be avoided if one did not allow oneself to love. At the time, it had been sound reasoning, and Meagan had found herself obeying it without conscious thought. Without her husband, she was suddenly alone in dealing with life's challenges as the thought to remarry seemed as preposterous as the sun rising in the west. In simple terms, life had kept her busy, kept her from forging relationships with her neighbours.

And yet, when she had needed them, they had come to save her.

In all fairness, it had been Lady Ainsworth, Derek's high-born wife, who had not hesitated. Since her husband had been taken ill, she had sent word to her neighbours for help before rushing to the cabin herself, saving little Erin and injuring herself in the process.

As Huntington House was still in a sad condition after the last baron had gambled away its wealth, Derek and his family were forced to do most of the work necessary themselves. However, as people of the working class, they had never expected or hoped for riches. More than once, Meagan had seen pride in their eyes as they went about restoring the old estate. As a man true to his word, Derek had not hesitated to roll up his sleeves and assist his tenants in repairing their ramshackle homes. Thus, he had gained their respect and loyalty, bringing them all closer together.

Only Meagan had not expected that their loyalty would extend to her.

But it had, and she had come to understand that a life lived alone was a sad existence. She did not want that for her children.

After they had been taken in at Huntington House, Meagan had come to realise the comfort of companionship, of family. Not only was Derek's mother Bessy a mother to all living under her roof, but Meagan had found close friends in Derek's wife Madeline and sister Kara. Social standing did not matter at Huntington House, and although his tenants referred to him as *my lord*, Meagan had seen him cringe at the address more than once. Tonight, everyone was invited to the grand house for a Christmas Eve supper, and for the first time since her husband's death, Meagan was looking forward to the holidays.

Edward's loss still made her heart ache, but by now she had come to realise that her children's joy possessed the power to heal it.

A little bit every day.

"Will we live at the big house now?" Matthew asked, coming to stand beside her.

Patting his head, Meagan smiled. "For a little while. But our neighbours have promised to help us rebuild, remember? Before spring is out, ye will sleep in your own bed again."

Grinning, Matthew looked up at her. "Will there be a tree right next to the house?"

Meagan laughed, "Do ye see a tree?"

Shaking his head, Matthew's gaze darkened.

"Fine," Meagan sighed. "Maybe we can plant a tree." A deep smile came to Matthew's face. "But only a small one."

"Thank ye, Mother," Matthew exclaimed, throwing his arms around her.

"I want a tree, too!" Little Erin stated, pulling on Meagan's skirts to get her attention. "I want a tree, too."

Meagan smiled. "We'll see." For now, she was grateful for the people in her life, for a wonderful Christmas with her family and a new home come spring.

Never again would she allow herself to retreat from the world. It had been a mistake. She knew that now. And she would never do so again.

After all, she had never been one to go quietly in the night. No, deep down, Meagan knew she was a fighter, and she would do whatever necessary to see her children happy.

Was not that what a mother did?

Chapter Three
RETURNING HOME

After the rain, the roads were soaked, littered with puddles that were slowly turning the dry earth into mud. Water dripped off branches, swirling through the air, travelling on the strong wind that seemed to howl like a wild beast.

After spending the past few months scraping together every coin he came by, Edward had finally been able to find passage on a ship back home. Back to England.

And this was his welcome.

Maybe it was the universe's way of telling him that he, in fact, was no longer welcome. Maybe this had been a mistake. Maybe he ought to turn back.

But he could not.

Dragging himself onward, Edward cursed as his left foot splashed through yet another puddle, soaking his pant leg higher. He inhaled a deep breath and glanced ahead at the small road winding its way through the country.

Never had he been in these parts before. Not since he had left for the war. And yet, it all felt familiar. The landscape. The sound of incessant raindrops drumming down onto the earth. The smell of rain and mud and dirt in the air.

Edward's whole body hummed with a sense of recognition, of being back home.

Again, he cursed. He should never have come.

And yet, he continued onward, forcing one foot in front of the other, ignoring the rumbling of his stomach, trying his best to forget that it had been three days since he had last eaten. Pulling his coat tighter around his shoulders to keep in what little warmth he possessed, he absentmindedly ran a hand over his chin, feeling the wild growth of his beard. If he were to come upon his family, would they even recognise him?

As the landscape began to change and Edward found himself remembering certain twists and turns of the road as well as the skyline before his eyes, he wondered how to best avoid such an unfortunate encounter. For if he were to stumble upon his family and they did not recognise him, Edward was certain it would tear his heart into a million pieces.

For the hundredth time, he cursed himself for embarking on such a foolish endeavour. He ought to have flung himself off the cliff when he had still had the chance.

When the first few puffs of smoke came into view, Edward stopped, taking a deep breath as his heart hammered in his chest the same way it had on the day he had first laid eyes on his wife. They had been children then, and still, he had known her to be the one.

As though Fortune had willed it.

After glancing around, Edward ventured off the path that led into the small village. Instead, he turned east, dragging his useless leg through soaked meadows and up a small slope. Panting under his breath, he continued upward, feeling a slight dizziness engulf his senses. His grip on his cane tightened, and he willed himself not to stop. If he did, he was not certain he would find the strength to start walking again.

Then the top came into view, and Edward gritted his teeth, taking the last few final steps before his gaze dropped, following the slight slope downward to the village snuggled into the small valley. Smoke rose from the chimneys, and here and there, Edward spotted a few brave souls bracing the outdoors. A few boys ran across the market square, and a farmer or two tended to their livestock.

Squinting his eyes, Edward shifted his gaze to the west. At the sight of his old home, the breath caught in his throat and he stumbled backward a pace as though someone had punched him in the stomach.

All these years, he had spent envisioning his family, his home. And now, it was only a short walk away.

Tears streamed down his face as his one good knee gave out and he sank down into the wet grass. For how long, Edward sat there, staring at his former home, he did not know.

As evening fell, he found himself jarred out of his trance when the door to his cottage opened and a little boy came running out, followed by a large dog.

"Matthew," Edward whispered, staring wide-eyed at the brown-haired boy.

Slowly, he dragged himself to his feet, his gaze unwavering, as his body leaned forward, unable to tear himself from the allure before him. How tall his son had grown? He mused for a moment before a burly man came hurtling through the door, yelling something unintelligible and pointing toward the barn.

Once again, Edward felt as though the air was knocked from his lungs as he stared at the man who had replaced him.

Although he had spent the better part of the journey across the channel convincing himself that his wife had remarried, Edward now knew all his preparations had done him little good. Now faced with the life he had given up, the life that had been claimed by another man, Edward felt a wild rage surging through his body. Gripping his cane, he began staggering down the small slope.

Then he once more stopped in his tracks as the door to the cottage opened, revealing a tall woman with dark-brown hair. For a moment, she hesitated, her gaze sweeping across her surroundings before she finally stepped outside...followed by two half-grown girls.

"'Tis not Meagan," Edward whispered before his gaze once more travelled to the little boy. Squinting his eyes, he tried to make out his features. "'Tis not him." Shaking his head, Edward felt his breath come in ragged gasps as his heart filled with a mixture of relief and fear. "'Tis not them," he mumbled, still staggering toward the family that quite obviously now lived in his old home. "Where are they?"

As he approached the small homestead, the burly man caught sight of him and stepped forward, his shoulders squared and a tense expression on his features. Then he gestured for his family to head inside before he took a step toward Edward. "Can I help ye?"

Blinking, Edward realised how close he had come to the family without offering a greeting. "I apologise," he said to the burly man, swallowing the lump in his throat. "I'm lookin' for…the Dunning family. They used to live here."

The burly man's eyes narrowed as he surveyed Edward, taking in his bedraggled appearance. "What is it to ye?" he demanded, arms crossed in front of his body.

Edward drew in a steadying breath as impatience burnt in his veins. Still, he forced himself to remain calm. "I've just returned from the continent," he spoke honestly before he switched to a lie. "I'm here to fulfil a promise I gave to Mr. Dunning. He died in the war, and he bade me speak to his family on his behalf."

At his words, the expression in the man's eyes softened. "I was told that the family who used to live here was called Dunning. A mother and two children."

Edward sucked in a sharp breath, feeling his chest tighten. "Matthew and Erin?"

The other man nodded, the last sign of doubt leaving his face. "Aye."

"Do ye know where they are? What happened to them?"

The burly man shrugged. "I was told they'd moved away. 'Tis all I know." Then he jerked his chin in the direction of the village in his back. "Go and ask Mr. Bradley at the tavern. If anyone knows, 'tis him."

Swallowing, Edward nodded. "Thank ye." And without another word, he hobbled past his old home and toward the market square where the tavern was located.

Except for his own home, few things had changed. A handful of houses had risen from the ground to house new families, but apart from that, the village looked as it always had.

As though no time had passed.

And yet, nothing could be farther from the truth.

Pushing open the heavy door to the small establishment, Edward welcomed the slight warmth that engulfed him after sleeping out in the open for the past few weeks. Then he glanced around, remembering the regular-sized room with a few tables scattered around the fireplace in the back. Toward the side wall, a counter had been set up, behind which Trevor-Mr. Bradley-was polishing a glass to perfection, his small, beady eyes sizing Edward up.

For a moment, Edward held his breath, hoping the man would not recognise him. However, they had not known each other well, and after Edward had married Meagan, the other man had avoided him openly, begrudging Edward his beautiful bride.

"Can I help ye?" Trevor asked, his eyes still watchful.

Approaching, Edward kept his gaze down, grateful for the beard that hid the lower half of his face. "I'm lookin' for the Dunning family," he answered as before. "I was told they'd moved away." Seeing Trevor's suspicious gaze, Edward added, "I served in the war with Mrs. Dunning's husband."

"I see," Trevor grumbled as though he even now begrudged Edward his wife when he surely thought him dead.

"Do ye know what happened?" Edward asked, sinking onto a barstool, his limbs sighing in relief.

Trevor took a deep breath and for a long moment said nothing. Then he shrugged, and an oddly familiar look of boredom settled on his features. "About a year after Mr. Dunning was reported dead, Derek McKnight returned."

Derek! Edward sighed in relief. He would have looked after them. His friend would have made certain that-

"He's been made a baron." Shaking his head, Trevor chuckled; however, there was a hostile tone to his laughter. "Distinguished himself in the field, they say." Again, he shook his head. "Was given an estate." He snorted, setting down the glass with a loud *bang*. "Came to collect Meagan and the children to live at his fine estate with him." A touch of anger came to his eyes. "If I'd known that's all it took, I would've gone off to war as well as claim her for myself."

"Claim her?" Edward echoed, staring at the man he had known and despised all his life.

Blinking, Trevor focused his gaze on him. "Why else would a man make such an offer? Why else would she accept it?" Shaking his head, Trevor leaned forward conspiratorially. "Mark my words: first, he left his friend for dead, and then he stole his wife."

As the blood rushed in his ears, Edward gripped the side of the counter, doing his utmost to steady himself as his body began to sway with the blow of such a revelation. Had Derek truly come back to—?

Shaking his head, Edward tried to clear it of the images such thoughts brought forth. "Where?" he stammered. "Where's the estate?"

"It's got some mighty fine name," Trevor scoffed, scratching his chin. "Huntington House, yeah, that's it. South-east of here."

"Thank ye," Edward stammered before he fled back out into the fresh air, leaving behind the suffocating tavern with a sigh of relief. Outside, a mild drizzle fell, wetting his face and chilling his bones. Was it true? Had his best friend claimed his wife? Never had Derek shown any interest in Meagan. Neither had she shown any in him. But these things did happen, did they not? After all, they thought him dead.

Is this not what you wanted? A voice deep down whispered. *Is this not the answer you sought?*

Gritting his teeth, Edward knew that he ought to turn back. After all, no matter what had happened between his best friend and his wife, Edward was certain that Derek would take care of her and his children. Was it not good that Matthew and Erin had a father in their lives? A man who would put their well-being before his own? Deep down, Edward knew that Derek would have never left for the war had he had a wife and child. He would not have abandoned them, and he would not abandon Meagan and the children. They were safe with him.

And that was all that mattered, wasn't it?

Still, Edward was powerless against the seething rage that gripped his heart as he contemplated the thought of his wife in the arms of his best friend. Although he had his answer, he could not simply bow out. He could not leave without...

Without what?

Drawing in a deep breath, Edward focused his eyes on the far horizon, almost invisible in the darkening sky. Then he turned toward the small chapel, hoping for sanctuary for the night, because tomorrow he would get on the road heading south-east.

Cursing under his breath, Edward knew that he should have thrown himself off the cliff when he had still had the chance. Now, it was too late.

Now, he had to see them.

Her.

And Heaven help him once he did.

Chapter Four
A GHOST COME HOME

As the new year progressed, Meagan delighted in seeing her new neighbours get to work on rebuilding her home. Although she had argued that their own homes ought to come first, they had insisted that she needed a place of her own to raise her children.

Never had Meagan felt so overcome with emotions of gratitude and pride as these people-people she hardly knew-set everything else aside to help her. In the following weeks as spring brought forth blooming flowers and trees and bushes, Meagan slowly got to know them.

Men devoted to providing for their families.

Women dedicated to caring for their children.

And little boys and girls-like her own-determined to explore life to the fullest.

As Meagan found her place among them, her past slowly receded, and she realised that although her heart would never heal completely, life still held love and wonder and beauty. And her children deserved no less.

Neither did she.

"How much longer is it?" she asked Kara, Derek's younger sister, as they sat in the drawing room of Huntington House. "Ye look about ready to burst."

Kara smiled, brushing a gentle hand over her swollen belly. "Mother says maybe a week or two."

"Are you hoping for a girl or a boy?" Madeline, Derek's wife, asked, glancing up from her embroidery.

Kara shrugged. "I could not say. Sometimes I think it'd be nice to have a daughter, but then I look at Collin and know that having another son would also be a dream come true."

Meagan smiled as she squinted her eyes at the fine stitches before her. "I know what ye mean. Before Erin was born, I felt the same way. Just ye wait until ye hold your new babe in your arms." Looking up, she met Kara's eyes. "As soon as ye do, ye will not be able to imagine having any other child than the one right before your eyes."

Sighing, Kara leaned back, glancing at her swollen belly with awe shining in her eyes. "I do believe you're right, Meagan." Then she lifted the small nightdress she was sewing for the baby and set back to work. "At least, I'll have a little more time to finish these," she chuckled. "Every day counts." Then she glanced up, and her eyes narrowed. "Although I could do without the constant shadow."

Following her gaze, Meagan and Madeline laughed. "He is only concerned about you," Madeline exclaimed as she saw her brother-in-law, Kara's husband Sean, walking by the doorway for the hundredth time that day. Glancing in, his eyes met Kara's before he hurried along, clearly afraid she would scold him once more.

Meagan smiled, touched by the silent devotion Sean showed towards his wife. Over the past months, he had barely left her side-only when forced-keeping a watchful eye on the mother of his children.

"I think he remembers Collin's birth better than I do," Kara mumbled, eyes fixed on the needle in her hand. "I do remember that it was painful, but mostly, all I see in my mind is that little boy in my arms, his little fingers curled around mine." Smiling wistfully, she brushed a hand over her belly. "I loved him instantly."

Meagan sighed, "I suppose for husbands 'tis different." Then she looked up and glanced from Kara to Madeline. "Would ye say 'tis worse to feel pain or to see someone ye love go through it?"

"I'd rather take it on myself than see my children suffer," Kara instantly replied. "Somehow that's easier...and less painful."

Meagan nodded. "I agree."

For a moment, Madeline remained silent, her gaze distant as she seemed to consider their words. With no children of her own just yet, she had no way of truly understanding their words. "Even though I'm not a mother," she finally said, a touch of regret in her dark green eyes, "I do believe you're right. It was agonising to see Derek suffer when he was sick. I know it is different because he's my husband and not my child, but still..."

Kara nodded. "Yes, you're absolutely right." Again, she glanced out the doorway. "I know it's why he stays close by, and he's right. When the baby comes, I want him by my side." She drew in a deep breath. "I will need him by my side."

Smiling, Madeline reached over and squeezed her sister-in-law's hand, their eyes meeting, saying more than a thousand words ever could.

Inhaling deeply, Meagan turned back to her own work, blinking back the tears that threatened as she saw the women's love for their husbands. Although she wished them nothing but happiness, sometimes the silent joy they felt at their husbands' attentions and softly whispered words only served to remind her that she herself would never again be at the receiving end of such love.

Only too well did she remember the hum in the air when she had caught her husband's meaningful glance from across the table. Only too well did she remember his thoughtfulness when he brought in water from the well before setting to work. Only too well did she remember the soft caress of his breath on her neck when he pulled her into his arms from behind when she least expected it.

But that was all they were now: memories.

Nothing more.

Footsteps echoed closer, and Meagan looked up, seeing Kara roll her eyes as she turned to the doorway.

As expected, Sean appeared, his posture rather stiff as he carried himself with an unusual air of formality. Giving a slight nod of the head, he looked to Madeline. "My lady, you have a visitor."

Glancing at each other, Meagan saw equal looks of surprise come to the other two women's faces. "A visitor?" Madeline enquired. "Did he give a name?"

His shoulders tense, Sean shook his head. "Should I send him away?"

For a moment, Madeline hesitated, her eyes watchful as they remained fixed on Sean's face, trying to gauge his assessment of the stranger. Then she sighed and put down her embroidery. "No, bid him inside."

"I shall." Holding her gaze a moment longer, Sean turned down the hall, returning within a short moment with a haggard man on his heels.

Dressed in work-worn clothes, the stranger appeared in the doorway, his face overgrown with a shaggy beard, his long hair unkempt as he leaned heavily on a cane, his left leg unnaturally straight as though he could not bend it at the knee. However, it was the coldness in his eyes that sent a shiver down Meagan's back.

The man's eyes travelled around the room, from face to face, and then, for a reason she did not know, they settled on hers.

Held hers.

Burned into hers.

Swallowing, Meagan found herself looking back at him, unable to avert her eyes. She noticed the slight tremble in his shoulders, the hard set of his jaw as well as the knuckles of his right hand, gripping the cane so tightly, making them stand out white.

There was something oddly familiar about this man.

And yet, he did not *look* familiar.

Meagan could have sworn she had never seen him before.

And yet, ...

...there was something in the air as they looked into each other's eyes.

Something that made her catch her breath.

Something that sent her heart into an uproar.

Something that-

"My congratulations on your marriage, my lady," the stranger spoke, interrupting her thoughts. Although his words were usually uttered to express well-wishes, Meagan had no trouble discerning the hatred and abhorrence dripping from them.

And then it hit her!

"My lady?" Meagan mumbled, frowning as she glanced at Madeline, who kept looking back and forth between Meagan and the stranger. Had he just called her *my lady*? Why would he?

Barely noting the dark frown that came to Sean's face as he stood at the ready in case the situation was to develop in an unwanted direction, Meagan found herself the centre of attention. All eyes were focused on her as the stranger's words echoed in her mind.

Not the words, no.

But his voice.

A voice she had never thought to hear again.

A voice she had longed to hear nonetheless.

Out of the corner of her eye, Meagan saw Madeline rise to her feet and take a step toward the man in the doorway. "Thank you," she said, her voice steady. "That is very kind of you, sir. May I enquire as to your name?"

As her eyes were still fixed on the stranger, Meagan saw a touch of confusion come to his eyes at Madeline's words. He swallowed, and for a moment, his stare wavered before it found hers once more. Only now, the dark brown of his eyes held no hatred, no darkness.

Now, all she saw was pain and loss and regret.

And in that instant, her heart made the final leap her mind could not.

Edward, it said, and the tears she had held back for so long spilled down her cheeks as she stared at the ghost before her.

It could not be! This was a trick! A hallucination! Was she losing her mind?

Sometimes she would see him in her dreams; however, they were always memories of the past. And it had been a long time since she had thought to hear his voice, only to turn and see that it was not him who had spoken.

Glancing at the other two women, Meagan knew that he was not an apparition. He could not be, for they saw him as well, did they not?

It was not only she. Or had she strayed into a dream without noticing? Was she asleep? Would she wake any second now to find the other side of the bed empty?

Swallowing, Meagan closed her eyes, remembering the mornings she had awoken from her dreams to have reality rushing back, slamming into her with such force that she almost doubled over, feeling her heart bleed with the remembered loss of what could never be again.

Her hands began to tremble as she remembered the pain, the consequences of false hope and the distant thought that she would not be able to go on without her husband. That thought had terrified her beyond anything she had ever imagined, and it had taken more strength than she thought she would have to return from the abyss of despair.

Shaking her head, Meagan felt all blood drain from her face as an old cold spread through her. Fear. Panic. Terror.

No, she would not be able to pull herself from the abyss again. If she allowed herself to believe that he had returned-against all odds-and it proved false-again! -she would not be able to survive.

Staring across the room at the haggard man, Meagan forced her mind into a different direction. Maybe it was not him. Maybe he only resembled her husband. Maybe...

Was he truly here?

"Are you all right?" Madeline asked, deep concern on her face as she hastened to Meagan's side. Sitting down beside her, she grasped her hands, her green eyes searching her friend's face.

Staring back and forth between Madeline and...and...

What was she to say? How could she even begin to explain...? Did she even need to? After all, this was a dream, was it not? Why could she not wake up? This was torture. Seeing her husband so close, and yet, knowing she could never reach him was the worst kind of torture.

He was only a memory. Nothing more.

"Would you tell us your name?" Sean addressed...the man..., whose eyes were hard as he glanced at the women in the room. "Otherwise, I must insist that you leave this instant."

However, her husband remained silent, his gaze locked on Meagan's, and in that moment, she felt the familiar hum in the air that had been absent from her life for too long. A sob escaped her, and her heart thudded so rapidly in her chest that she feared it might collapse with exhaustion.

He's alive! It screamed, its deafening sound ringing in Meagan's ears.

Overwhelmed by the onslaught of emotions, Meagan shot to her feet, feeling cornered, her gaze drifting to the side entrance which led to the back of the house.

A way out.

Shaking her head, she backed away, her eyes still fixed on her husband. Her husband! "Ye're alive," she stammered, staring at him with wide eyes. "How can ye…? No, ye can't. 'Tis not real. It can't be." Retreating from the threat to her heart standing so close, Meagan felt all the pieces of her newly constructed life come crashing down around her, stripping away the confident woman she had become, the wisdom she had gained, the life lessons she had learnt. "'Tis a dream," she whispered, her voice sounding choked even to her own ears. "It cannot be so." Staring into his eyes, Meagan felt like a young girl again, afraid to show how she felt lest he not return her feelings, afraid her heart would break yet again and rob her of her will to live. "Edward," she whispered, feeling her body tremble as his name tumbled from her lips.

"What?" Madeline gasped, her eyes going wide as she stared at Meagan.

Swallowing, Meagan met her gaze, a soft smile coming to her face as though seeking to put her friend at ease. This was not real, was it? Still, she heard herself say, "He's my husband."

Madeline's mouth opened and closed as her gaze shifted to the stranger standing stock-still in the doorway. "But…how…?"

Meagan closed her eyes, and instantly, her mind was flooded with a myriad of questions, overwhelming her once more. As bright spots began to dance before her eyes and blind panic flooded her being, her survival instinct kicked in.

Fighting to keep upright despite the sense of upheaval in her head, she turned and fled the room.

Chapter Five
BEHIND A NAME

Staring after his wife, Edward felt as though the air had been knocked from his lungs. His knees felt weak, and the exhaustion of the past months caught up with him. Swaying on his feet, he gripped his cane, willing himself to remain upright.

Meagan, his heart whispered, and an unbidden smile tugged at the corners of his mouth. It had been so long since he had last seen her, and the conjured images of her in his mind could not hold a candle to the woman of flesh and blood he had loved all his life, the woman he had seen with his own eyes only a moment ago.

Her golden hair and pale blue eyes had bewitched him as they first had over a decade ago. She had lost nothing of her loveliness, of the generous character underneath her friendly face and kind eyes. And although he had allowed his anger to guide him, afraid of her influence on him, he still had felt compelled to sweep her into his arms the moment he had laid eyes on her.

If only.

Taking a deep breath, Edward finally became aware of the fact that the remaining people in the room were staring at him, a rather dumbfounded expression on all their faces. Who were they? Edward wondered for the first time since he had arrived at Huntington House.

Drawing in a deep breath, the raven-haired woman approached him, her dark green eyes searching his face. "You're Meagan's husband?" she asked, a touch of awe in her voice as though she did not dare believe it.

Edward swallowed. Was he? Still? He had been...once. But now...

Still, unable to stop himself, he felt his head bob up and down, rejoicing in the acknowledgement.

The dark-haired woman swallowed before a deep smile came to her face. Then she sobered, and her head jerked to the man still standing by Edward's side. "Sean, go and fetch Derek. Now!"

At the sound of his friend's name, Edward cringed. What had he been thinking coming here? Now, he would not only have to face his wife, but also his best friend. Former best friend, Edward corrected himself.

"You're Edward Dunning?" the woman asked, her gaze holding his.

Again, Edward nodded.

Glancing behind her at the other woman, who stared at him with an equally stunned expression in her eyes, she took a step toward him. "It is nice to meet you. I'm Lady Ainsworth, Derek's wife."

For the second time that day, Edward felt as though he would topple over. As Lady Ainsworth's words as well as their implications sank into his mind and heart, he felt his knees give out.

His cane dropped to the ground with a loud clatter, and stumbling sideways, Edward braced himself with his shoulder against the door frame, slowly sinking to the floor, his left leg stretched out before him. Panting under his breath, he stared at the dark-haired woman, who knelt beside him, her eyes wide with concern as she spoke to him.

However, Edward could not make out a single word.

Meagan.

He shook his head. She was not married! At least not to Derek. She was...She was still his, wasn't she?

Closing his eyes, Edward exhaled all the tension of the past weeks. Although he never once had thought of such an outcome, he could not deny the joy it brought to his heart. And yet, he wondered why it would. After all, he had no intention of staying. For the truth remained unchanged: although she was his, he did not deserve her, and if he stayed, he would only ruin the life she had built here for herself and their children.

Matthew. Erin. Where were they?

A deep desire to see them burnt in his chest, and it was in that moment that he knew he had to leave. If he were to see them...and her, he would not have the strength to set them free.

Reaching for his cane, Edward held on to the door frame as he slowly-excruciatingly slowly-pulled himself back up onto his feet. However, the moment he turned to the front hall, the door opened, and Derek strode in.

As Derek's eyes fell on him, his friend stopped short, his jaw tensing as he stared. "Edward," he mumbled, his voice laced with disbelief. Rubbing his hands over his face, Derek shook his head. Then he came toward him, his eyes shifting over Edward's face, before Edward found himself crushed in a tight embrace.

Taken aback, Edward froze, barely noting the two women and the man named Sean leaving the room. How long had it been since anyone had hugged him? Touched him? Shown him any sign of affection?

Closing his eyes, Edward leaned into his friend, feeling slight stirrings in his heart as it remembered the joys of love and friendship, of devotion and loyalty. In answer, his left arm came up and returned the embrace with all the strength he had left in him.

"I thought you were dead," Derek whispered beside his ear, still holding on as though afraid Edward would slip away if he were to let go.

"As did I."

Finally stepping back, Derek kept a hand on Edward's left shoulder. "What happened?" he asked, his dark eyes searching his friend's face.

"I was injured," Edward said, sinking back against the door frame, as he conjured some of the worst memories of his life, "and left behind. Later, I found my name on a casualty list."

A deep frown came to Derek's face. "When was that?"

Meeting his friend's gaze, Edward swallowed. "Two years ago."

"Two years ago," Derek repeated, shaking his head. "I was told you had fallen two years ago." Not saying another word, Derek held his gaze, a clear question in them.

Edward drew in a deep breath. "I need to go." There was no use in prolonging the inevitable.

"Go?" Derek frowned. "Where?"

Edward shrugged. "Back."

Derek's gaze narrowed, and a suspicious gleam came to his dark depth. "You do not plan on staying," he accused, his voice hardening.

Edward shook his head. "I only came to…"

"To what?" Derek dared him, annoyance now clear in his voice. "Why did you come?"

Gritting his teeth, Edward met his friend's accusing stare. "I was told you had come to…claim her," he hissed, feeling his insides twist and turn at the memory.

Snorting, Derek shook his head. "I meant before. Why did you return to England if all you want to do is leave?"

Averting his gaze, Edward made to step past his friend, but Derek's arm shot out, blocking his path. As he looked up, he found his oldest friend's hard eyes on him.

"Do you truly think I will simply let you walk out of here?" Slowly, Derek shook his head. "Meagan deserves better than that."

Edward nodded. "I agree, and that is exactly why I have to go."

Their eyes remained locked as Derek's gaze narrowed, his watchful eyes assessing, contemplating, searching. "What makes you say that?"

Edward sighed, exhaustion weighing heavily on his shoulders. It had been years since he had spoken to another soul the way he had in the past few minutes. Ever since he had arrived on the continent and he and Derek had gone their separate ways, assigned to different regiments, Edward had lived in his head mostly, carrying conversations with people who were not there.

"Talk to me," Derek insisted, his gaze drilling into Edward's as he came to stand before him, hands clasped on his friend's shoulders, a clear sign that he had no intention of allowing him to simply walk away. "We've known each other all our lives, and I've never known you to give up. What changed?"

Edward swallowed, "I'm a different man now than I was then," he began, attempting to put the turmoil in his heart into words. "Or maybe I've always been this man I am now, only it was the war that made me see it, realise it." He shrugged, feeling his muscles strain slightly against the extra burden of his friend's hands on his shoulders. "Whatever the reason, the truth remains."

"What truth?"

Taking a deep breath, Edward steeled himself for the pain he knew would be his. "I'm a selfish man. First and foremost, I think only of myself, of what I want. Not even my family's needs I was able to put before my own. I'm the lowest of men."

Shaking his head, Derek stared at him thunderstruck. "Why would you say that? Why would you think that? Do you believe a woman like Meagan would ever love you if that were true?"

Edward's heart skipped a beat at his friend's words. "Maybe I misled her. Maybe she couldn't see it because I couldn't either." He sighed, "But I do now, and I know that if I stay, she will suffer for it as she has suffered at my selfish decisions before." Gritting his teeth, he shook his head. "The way she is suffering now. You asked me why I came back. Well, I had to see her. That's the answer. And now she will have to face the consequences when I leave again. She mourned me once; now she will have to do it again."

"Then stay!" Derek snapped, his shoulders tense, his gaze troubled. "Don't put her through this!"

Edward shook his head. "I cannot."

"Why?"

"Because I have no right to," Edward snapped, his hand clenched around his cane, his muscles aching with the tension that held his body rigid. "When I left, I forfeited every right I might have once had to her. I gave up my family, the life we had. I sacrificed it all to…be someone, to distinguish myself." Shaking his head, Edward groaned at the memory of his foolishness. "I have no right to reclaim them now."

For a long moment, Derek remained silent, his watchful eyes gliding over Edward's face. "And what about her? What about what she wants? Losing you nearly destroyed her. However, Meagan is not a woman to give up easily. She fought her way back into life. She still is."

Edward nodded. "Believe me, I know how strong she is, and I'm sorry she had to be. But she will be better off without me."

Derek shook his head. "She still loves you the way she's always loved you. You have no right to do this to her all over again." He scoffed, "I guess you were right. You shouldn't have come. But you did, and now, you cannot simply leave." Leaning back, a smirk came to Derek's face as he held Edward's gaze. "She won't let you."

Edward inhaled a slow breath, knowing only too well that his friend was right. If there ever had been a woman to fight with no regard for herself, it was Meagan. Always had she known with absolute certainty what she wanted, what was best for her family, and if she believed that what was best for them was him, then he would not get away.

The touch of a smile came to Edward's face as he felt his resolve begin to waver.

And it terrified him more than anything ever had.

Chapter Six
ALIVE

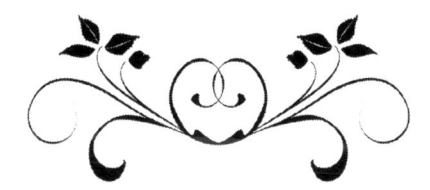

Walking up the slope to the small mount from where she could gaze down at her new cottage, Meagan sighed. The repairs were well on their way, and only a few improvements remained. Soon, she and her children would be able to return home.

And Edward? Her mind whispered.

Shaking her head, Meagan rubbed her hands over her eyes, terrified that all this had merely been a dream, that she would wake up any moment and realise that he was truly gone.

How often had this happened before? How often had she dreamed of her husband's return, only to awaken and find reality still as it had been before she had gone to sleep?

A few weeks after learning of his death, Meagan had begun to dream of him. At first, these dreams had only been small memories of him smiling at her or holding little Erin or carrying Matthew on his shoulders. Then over time, the dreams had grown into complex scenarios. It had almost been as though she had had two lives. One with her children during the day, and another one that included her husband during the night. After a while, Meagan had found herself unwilling to get up in the morning, wishing to return to the beautiful world the rising sun forced her to leave behind. It had been then that she had realised that she could not go on like this any longer.

She had to let him go.

And it had broken her heart to do so.

Swallowing, Meagan glanced over her shoulder at the manor house she had fled. Had it been a dream, or not? Was her husband truly in that house? Only a short walk away?

A soft breeze, still cold from the last memories of winter, brushed over her, chilling her skin and making her shiver. Wrapping her arms around herself, Meagan kept looking back and forth between her cottage and the manor house. It was as though she found herself at a crossroad.

If he was truly here, where would their future lie?

Remembering the hatred and disappointment in her husband's eyes, Meagan cringed. At first, she had been too overwhelmed to understand why he would look at her thus. However, now, after repeatedly replaying the moment in the drawing room in her mind, Meagan finally understood.

My congratulations on your marriage, my lady.

Closing her eyes, Meagan inhaled a deep breath. He thought she had married his best friend. How could he think that of her? How could he assume-?

"You look cold."

Spinning around, Meagan breathed a sigh of relief when she saw it was Madeline striding toward her, a warm coat draped over her arm.

"Here, take this," Madeline said, holding out the coat to Meagan and helping her slip it on. "How do you feel?"

Staring at her friend, Meagan felt her mouth open and close before she merely shook her head. "I cannot say."

Madeline nodded. "I suppose I wouldn't, either. I cannot imagine what it must be like seeing him again after believing him dead for so long."

Pressing her lips into a tight line, Meagan felt tears run down her cheeks.

"This is not how you imagined the moment of your husband's return, is it?"

Jerking her head sideways, Meagan stared at Madeline. "How do you know?" she asked, trying to remember if she had ever spoken to her friend about her dreams.

Madeline smiled. "If it had been Derek, I would have. Honestly, I cannot imagine anyone not doing so."

Meagan sighed, realising how precious this new-found friendship was to her. "For a long time, I couldn't close my eyes without seein' him. He would come stridin' toward me with a smile on his face and love shinin' in his eyes, and he would sweep me into his arms and never let me go again."

Madeline nodded, a soft smile curving up her lips. "That sounds wonderful."

"It does." Remembering the moment in the drawing room, Meagan felt her heart sink as her hopes and dreams perished.

"You're disappointed," Madeline observed.

Meagan scoffed, "Of course, I'm disappointed! How could I not be?" Spinning around, she stared at Madeline. "He's alive! HE IS ALIVE! I keep sayin' it but I still cannot believe it to be true." Shaking her head, Meagan felt the world around her begin to spin as her heart began to break all over again. "It should all be so easy," she mumbled, "but 'tis not." Then she looked up at Madeline. "He thought I was ye."

Her friend nodded. "I noticed. After you left, I introduced myself." She held Meagan's gaze. "His knees buckled, and he sank to the floor."

Meagan swallowed.

"He was relieved," Madeline said, an encouraging smile on her face. "Like someone realising that his worst fear had not come to pass. He still loves you."

Meagan shook her head, remembering the dark look in her husband's eyes. "I do not know if that is true," she whispered, trying to sort through the chaos in her head. "He seems different, not like the man I used to know."

"Was that not to be expected?" Madeline asked. "After all he's been through, we can hardly expect him to remain the same man. Life changes us; is that not so? Are you still the same woman you were when he left?"

Considering her friend's words, Meagan shook her head. "I guess not."

"Then speak to him," Madeline urged. "Find out who he is now."

A cold shiver ran down Meagan's spine at the thought of meeting her husband. "What if...?"

"What if what?" Madeline asked, her kind eyes holding Meagan's as she placed a hand on her friend's, giving it a gentle squeeze.

"What if life has changed him so much that...that the man he is now is not the man I love?" Meagan whispered, feeling her heart constrict painfully at the thought. "What if he cannot love *me* any longer? At least not the woman I have become? What if findin' out who he is now only serves to destroy the memory I have of my husband? What if we cannot find our way back to each other?"

Taking both of Meagan's hands into her own, Madeline held her gaze, her own imploring. "I will not deny that there is a chance that might happen," she admitted. "However, I fervently believe that both of you will regret it for the rest of your lives if you do not try. You love him. You've spent years dreaming of his return. And from the way he reacted earlier, I'm certain your husband did the same."

An encouraging smile came to Madeline's face, and Meagan could not help but allow herself to be swept away by her friend's words.

"Now, you have a chance to get him back. The real him. The man of flesh and blood. Not only a memory. But if you do not try, then you will lose him for good." Nodding, Madeline smiled. "The only question is: do you want him back?"

Holding her friend's gaze, Meagan smiled, feeling her heart flood with an emotion she had thought lost to her.

"Then fight for him," Madeline urged. "Don't let him slip away."

As tears streamed down her face, Meagan nodded. "The moment Derek told me of ye, I knew I'd like ye."

Laughing, Madeline pulled her into her arms and held her tight, giving Meagan the strength she would need in the days to come.

Although she did not know her husband's intentions in coming to Huntington House-after all, he had thought her married to his best friend-Meagan finally knew her own.

She wanted him back.

And damn him if he had other plans.

Chapter Seven
REMNANTS OF AN OLD LIFE

Overwhelmed by the events of that day, Edward stared at his friend. "I know how determined she can be, but I cannot...I need to go. I will not put that decision on her. I-"

"No!" Stepping into his friend's path, Derek shook his head, a touch of a smirk on his otherwise serious face. "She will skin me alive if I allow you to escape."

The corners of Edward's mouth tugged up before he could prevent it. "But-"

Children's laughter echoed to his ears as a myriad of little footsteps stampeded down the hall.

Derek's face stilled before a satisfied smile came to his lips.

Seeing his friend's reaction, Edward froze, knowing exactly what it meant. *Matthew. Erin.* He mouthed.

In answer, his friend nodded before a moment later, three young children burst into the drawing room, two boys and a girl.

Edward's heart stopped as he stared at the older boy, recognising the three-year-old he used to carry around on his shoulders. Only now he seemed more mature, grown into a boy with laughing eyes and a kind smile, reminding Edward of his wife. He moved with purpose, all the chubbiness of a little child replaced by strong limbs that ached for adventure and excitement. "Uncle Derek," Matthew exclaimed, his eyes aglow with eagerness. "I found another tree. Will you come look?"

"I want to climb, too," the small blond-haired girl pouted, her little arms crossed defiantly over her chest as her braids bounced up and down on her shoulders. "Matt said I'm too young, but I ain't."

Edward almost toppled over as he stared at her little face, her azure-coloured eyes narrowed in an accusing gaze. *Erin*, his heart whispered, trying to see the baby he had held in his arms in the little girl before him.

"Hold on a moment, Matthew," Derek calmed, his gaze lifting to meet Edward's. "There's something-"

"Don't!" Edward interrupted, panic seizing his heart.

Instantly, all three children spun around to stare at him, and his heart clenched painfully as his daughter shrank back, her little hand reaching for her brother's.

"They deserve to know," Derek replied, his voice determined as he held Edward's gaze. "I know well the desire to run from something that utterly frightens one, but no matter what it is, it's always a mistake." Nodding for emphasis, he held Edward's gaze a moment longer before turning back to the children. "Collin," he addressed the other little boy about Erin's age, "go and find your parents. I need to speak with Matt and Erin."

Hesitating for a moment, Collin shrugged and then darted off toward the back of the house.

"What is it, Uncle Derek?" Matthew asked, eyeing Edward with apprehension, his hand wrapped protectively around his little sister's.

Despite the tension, Edward's heart swelled with pride. Meagan had done a marvellous job raising them. They were extraordinary, to say the least.

As Derek knelt, Edward thought his heart would jump out of his chest; so fast did it hammer inside his ribcage. "Listen," Derek said, his voice gentle, "you remember how a while ago your mother was told that your father had died in battle, don't you?"

Both their little heads bobbed up and down. "Mother said he is a hero," Matthew announced proudly, and Edward felt himself cringe. If that was what his family thought, they were in for a harsh disappointment. He should never have come.

"Well," Derek continued, "today we learnt that that was a mistake."

Matthew's little face puckered into a frown. "He was not a hero?"

Derek smiled. "He certainly was. No, the mistake was that…he did not die." For a moment, he held Matthew's gaze before looking at Erin, who stared back at him, confusion in her warm eyes. "He was injured and lost," Derek continued before glancing up at Edward, "but he has finally found his way home."

Holding his breath, Edward watched in horror as his children's heads slowly turned toward him, their eyes wide as they stared at the stranger before them. More than ever, Edward was aware of his bedraggled appearance, and he wished he had taken the time to shave before rushing into Huntington House. What would his children think of him?

While Erin continued to stare, her soft eyes almost expressionless as her mind raced to make sense of what she had been told, Matthew's gaze grew inquisitive. His eyes narrowed as they swept over Edward's face, a spark of hope in their brown depths. Then he took a step closer, his hand still wrapped around his sister's. "Father?" he whispered, a slight quirk coming to the left corner of his mouth.

Torn between running for the hills and crushing his children into his arms, Edward drew in a deep breath. Then he knelt as well, his left leg awkwardly stretched out before him, and brushed a hand over his bearded face, trying his best to smile as his emotions ran rampant. "Hello, Matthew. I'm truly happy to see ye," he glanced at Erin, "both of ye. And I'm sorry if my appearance frightens ye. I've been travellin' for a long while, and I didn't have the time to change and shave."

Matthew swallowed, "I'm not frightened." Staring at his father a moment longer, his eyes suddenly cleared, and a smile came to his face as though he had come to a decision. "Why did people think ye were dead, Father? Why did ye not tell them ye were not?"

Surprised by his son's questions as much as the eagerness in his voice, Edward swallowed, contemplating how best to answer. For a moment, he looked up at Derek, who merely shook his head, a pleased smile on his face. "Well," Edward began, grasping for words. "I was injured, and I wasn't awake when they found me and declared me dead. I could not tell them."

Matthew nodded, understanding clear in his eyes. Then he looked at his father's leg. "What is wrong with your leg?"

Edward sighed, "I can no longer bend it at the knee. It makes walking-and kneeling-a bit difficult."

Fascinated, Matthew took a step closer, his eyes examining his father's leg. Then he felt his own knee, stretching it, and tried to walk without bending it. "It sure is difficult," he observed, his gaze shifting back to his father, a touch of pride in his eyes that stole the breath from Edward's lungs.

"Can ye still run?" Matthew enquired, his gaze aglow with eager curiosity.

Edward drew in a deep breath. "I haven't tried," he admitted, ashamed to reveal his shortcomings to his son. Even if he was too young still, one day, he would be disappointed to have a father with such limitations, especially when his father had been the one to bring them onto himself.

"Can ye climb a tree?" Matthew continued, a deep smile coming to his little face as he took a step toward his father. "I used to climb the tree by our cottage every day until it fell in the storm." A tinge of sadness came to his eyes. "'Twas the perfect tree. There's none like it."

"Did you not just tell us that you found another?" Derek asked from behind.

Looking over his shoulder at his uncle, Matthew nodded, an encouraged smile tugging at the corners of his mouth. "'Tis not as good as the old one, but I think it'll be fun to learn how to climb it."

Smiling, Derek nodded. "Why don't you show it to your father?"

Again, Edward cringed, feeling his opportunity for departure retreat into the distance. Judging from the insistent look in his friend's eyes, he felt certain that Derek would not give him a chance to steal away any time soon. If at all.

Before Edward knew what was happening, he found himself hobbling down the stairs and rounding the manor house, following in his son's wake as the boy eagerly pointed out a tree among many toward the back of the estate. "Ain't it wonderful?" Matthew beamed as his eyes slid upward, from branch to branch, until they reached the top, gently swaying in the breeze.

Edward drew in a deep breath, contemplating what to say. However, before he could make up his mind, his son approached the tree and skillfully swung himself up onto the first branch, pride glowing in his warm eyes.

"I want to climb, too," Erin chirped beside Edward, her pale blue eyes shifting back and forth between her brother and him. "I want to climb, too," she repeated before one hand tugged on Edward's sleeve while the other pointed at her brother.

Overwhelmed, Edward sucked in a sharp breath, his gaze shifting to meet Derek's.

With an amused grin on his face, his friend merely shook his head, and Edward realised that he was on his own. Derek would not interfere, would not help him.

After all, he was not their father.

Turning to his little daughter, Edward caught sight of Meagan standing with Derek's wife not too far on a small slope, their faces turned toward him and the children.

As his heart sped up, Edward forced steady breaths down his lungs before he wrenched his gaze away and knelt in front of his daughter, looking into her little face. "I know ye want to climb, too, Erin." Her name on his tongue felt heavenly. When had he last spoken it out loud?

Ages ago.

Nodding her little head, Erin watched him carefully, her eyes round as she held his gaze, her own holding a touch of apprehension. However, she did not back away.

"'Tis no fun staying behind, is it?" he asked, noting a small stab in his heart when he remembered his own desire for adventure and what it had cost him.

His daughter shook her head. "Matt always gets to climb, but not me. 'Tis not fair."

Pushing all troubling thoughts aside, Edward nodded, feeling the sudden urge to reach out to her and pull her into the comfort of his arms. However, he did not. After all, who was he to her? Only a stranger. "I know 'tis not easy, little Erin," Edward replied, unable to keep himself from speaking her name. "But ye're not old enough yet." Her little shoulders slumped, and Edward wanted nothing more but to promise her the world if only she would smile again. "Listen, when your brother was younger, he wasn't allowed to climb, either. Soon, your arms and legs will be long enough, and then you'll be able to join him." A small spark of hope came to her blue eyes. "I will teach ye."

The moment the words left his lips, Edward froze, cursing himself for allowing his heart to speak such words. Was he not still intent on leaving? Shaking his head, he knew that every moment he stayed would only make it worse once he did leave.

Then stay, his heart whispered.

Gritting his teeth against the onslaught of hope that suddenly surged through his being, Edward rose to his feet. Out of the corner of his eye, he caught sight of his wife walking toward him, her eyes fixed on him, a soft smile-full of hope-shining on her face.

Instantly, panic seized him. Turning to Derek, he knew that his friend would never allow him to leave. However, in that moment, Edward could only think about putting a safe distance between himself and his family. "I'd rather return to the house," he said, noting the calculating frown that came to Derek's eyes, "and change and shave. I ought to have done so before but…"

Derek inhaled a slow breath before he nodded. "All right. Go on ahead. I shall be right there." He took a step closer, his hard gaze drilling into Edward's. "I swear if you think of taking off, I will hunt you down like a dog, do you understand?"

Nodding, Edward could not help but smile. "Ye've always had a way with words, my friend. I've missed ye."

Derek's gaze narrowed. "Do not try to distract me. I meant what I said."

"I know," Edward replied before he turned toward the house. Casting a hesitant glance over his shoulder, he took note of the disappointment that came to his wife's gaze as he walked away.

Coward, something deep inside him whispered, and yet, Edward could not still his feet. As much as he loved his family, he feared them nonetheless. Feared their love and the life they offered him.

"Father!"

Matthew's voice felt like a slap in the face, and Edward almost lost his step, leaning heavily on his cane to keep from falling. Once more glancing over his shoulder, he saw his son's face high up in the tree as he gazed down at Derek, listening to his words of comfort.

He's much better at this than me, Edward thought, wondering if he simply should keep walking...no matter what the consequences.

Chapter Eight
A WALK

Swallowing, Meagan stared after her husband as he hobbled away toward the house, leaning heavily on his cane as though his legs barely managed to hold him up. The sight of his injury pained her, and yet, it had been the look in his eyes that had sent an even deeper pain to her heart. More than anything, he seemed broken inside as though he carried a wound invisible to the naked eye.

A wound she feared would never heal.

Did he even want it to heal?

"He's overwhelmed," Derek spoke out beside her, his gaze shifting from his wife to her. "He was gone for so long, and I don't think he ever believed he would return."

Madeline nodded, slipping her arm through her husband's. "He seems haunted," she agreed, seeking Meagan's gaze. "He needs your help."

Meagan drew in a deep breath and wrenched her gaze away from the house once her husband had disappeared inside. Glancing at her son climbing down the tall tree, she met Derek's gaze. "He thought we were married," she whispered, careful not to speak too loudly so her children would not overhear. "He thought I was your wife."

Exchanging a glance with Madeline, Derek nodded. "I thought he did. Someone back home must have said something to him. Something that made him think so. After all, how else would he have known where to look for you?"

For a moment, Meagan closed her eyes, imagining the days her husband had spent believing her married to his best friend. The man she had known would never have believed such a thing. He would have known that he was the only one she had ever loved. The only one she *would* ever love.

Oh, how he had changed! At his core, was he even still the man who held her heart? Or had that man perished on the continent?

"I shall see to him," Derek promised, nodding to her. "Don't worry." Then he walked back toward the house, his wife by his side, their heads bent toward one another in confidence.

Meagan sighed. Once upon a time, she and Edward had been like that as well. Would they ever get it back?

Feeling a slight tug on her sleeve, Meagan looked down at her daughter. "Are ye all right, my sweet?" she asked, brushing a tender hand over Erin's blond head.

With wide eyes, her daughter stared at her. "Is that man truly our father?"

Inhaling deeply, Meagan nodded, a soft smile on her face as she knelt and drew her daughter into her arms. "He is, my sweet. I know ye don't remember him," she said before leaning back and meeting her daughter's eyes, "but he loves ye very much. And he's done what he could to return home to ye…to us."

"Mother! Mother!"

Lifting her head, Meagan watched her son jump from the lowest branch and land safely on the ground before sprinting toward her. "Father is back! Did ye see? He's back!" A glowing smile rested on his face, and eagerness bubbled under his skin, and in that moment, Meagan realised how much he had missed his father. Unlike Erin, he had memories of a man who had carried him around on his shoulders, chased him up and down the hill, tucked him into bed and told him stories of lands faraway.

No matter her own state of mind, her doubts and fears, Meagan knew that for her children she would have to find a way to mend whatever had broken within her husband. Although his body had returned, his mind and heart seemed to be struggling as though they wished for nothing more than an instant departure. Meagan could not say what it was, but there had been something in the way he had looked at her that had sent a cold fear through her body...as though he did not intend to stay.

Holding a hand out to each of her children, Meagan walked with them back to the house and bade them sit down on the settee in the drawing room. Then she took a chair opposite them and tried her best to answer the many questions they had.

"I cannot say what happened," she admitted, meeting her son's gaze openly. "Your father only just returned this mornin', and I haven't had a chance to speak to him...in detail."

"Uncle Derek said Father had been lost," Matthew informed her, a touch of pride in his brown eyes to be the only one with such information. "They thought he had died, and he was not awake to tell him he wasn't dead."

Meagan swallowed, trying to hide her emotions at the thought of how close her husband had come to dying. Even after she had believed him dead for over two years, the thought sent goose bumps up and down her arms and she felt sick in the pit of her stomach. "Yes, there must have been some mistake," she agreed, ignoring the nausea that threatened to rise in her throat. "I'm very sorry that it happened, that we were made to believe that he had died." Reaching out, she grasped her children's hands. "I know it wasn't easy for ye, and I'm proud that ye welcomed him back with open hearts."

While Erin looked somewhat forlorn, Matthew beamed with joy.

"I know that we're all happy that he's back," she continued, knowing that her children's expectations would likely soon be disappointed when they realised that their father was not the man he had once been. "However, ye must understand that your father has been through a lot. War changes a man in many ways that we might not be able to understand."

Matthew nodded. "He told me his leg is hurt. He cannot bend it."

"Yes, his leg was hurt," Meagan said, nodding to her son, "but that is not what I meant. There are worse injuries than those of the body.

Fear may live in his heart now, and that is somethin' that cannot be easily healed."

"What kind of fear?" Matthew asked, his little face scrunched up as his mind worked to understand.

Meagan shrugged. "I don't know. There are many different kinds. Do ye remember when we first arrived here and ye fell out of the tree?" Matthew nodded. "For weeks ye were afraid to go near it, and ye relived the moment ye fell again and again in your dreams."

Matthew sighed, his eyes overshadowed. "It felt like I was falling all over again. 'Twas just as bad as the first time."

Squeezing her son's hand, Meagan nodded. "Whatever your father has been through, it might still live in his dreams, and it will take great courage to overcome. We must be patient and not be disheartened if he seems different than we remember him." As she looked into her children's faces, their little heads bobbing up and down, Meagan could only hope that she herself possessed such strength. What if she could not recognise the man she had once loved in the man before her?

Looking at himself in the mirror, his face scrubbed clean, his beard shaved off, his hair cut and brushed neatly, Edward barely recognised himself. Although he had never truly seen his own dishevelled appearance beyond having it reflected in the eyes of others, he knew that the man who looked back at him in the mirror was not the man he had become.

Once, it had been him.

However, since then, a lot had happened, changing him in ways that ought to be visible, ought they not? And yet, as he stared at his face, Edward could not see the darkness he knew now lived in his heart. There was nothing to warn others, to alert them to the change he had undergone. Nothing to tell his family that he was no longer the man they remembered.

"Are you ready?" Derek asked beside him, gesturing toward the door. "Madeline said they're downstairs in the drawing room."

Edward swallowed. "I don't know if-"

"But I do," his friend interrupted, gently but insistently guiding him out the door. "I know you're afraid, but if you do not face them now, the apprehension will only get worse. It is better to meet it head-on."

Hobbling awkwardly down the stairs, Edward cringed at the thought of what his friend might think of him. Did he pity him? Edward did not dare look in his eyes. Maybe not knowing was preferable to the truth. *Then why did ye come?* A voice deep inside whispered. *Why did ye not fling yourself off the cliff?*

Stopping in front of the drawing room, Derek reached out to open the door. "You're not alone in this. Meagan is as frightened as you are. Don't forget that?" Then his friend swung open the door and all but pushed him inside, shutting him in with the family he had thought he would never see again.

Wide eyes turned to him, taking in his changed appearance.

While his children looked pleased, searching his face, Meagan stared at him in shock as though she had not truly realised before that very moment that he had returned. What would she think once she saw the man he had become deep within? Would she turn from him then?

Once again, Edward knew he ought to leave. Not only to spare them-and himself-the disappointment that was sure to come, but also to protect the beautiful memories they had once created together. Would they not also be tainted by the disappointments that awaited them? Would his selfish return not rob them of everything they held dear?

"Father," his son exclaimed, breaking the silence. "I do remember ye better now." With a child's honesty, Matthew rose from the settee and stepped toward him, a large smile on his face.

Edward nodded. "I believe ye. Again, I apologise for not shaving beforehand. However, I never meant to-" Swallowing, Edward broke off, realising that he had almost said too much.

Fatigue clawed at his mind, and despite the quick meal Derek had brought up to him, he felt his strength dwindling. His vision blurred, and his knees felt as though they would give in at any moment.

"Why don't you two go and visit Bessy in the kitchen?" he heard his wife say, her voice sounding strangely distant. "I need a moment to speak to your father."

Small feet shuffled past him, and Edward heard the door open and close. However, it was not until he felt his wife's hand come down to lay gently-almost hesitantly-on his arm that he realised he was wide awake.

His eyes flew opened, and his arm jerked back as though burnt. Staring at his wife, her own eyes wide with shock, Edward swallowed, his skin tingling with the familiar hum he had always felt when near her. Why had he not felt it before? Or had he simply not noticed?

"Why don't ye sit down?" Meagan suggested, her voice shaky as she gestured to the settee. "Ye look as though ye might keel over."

Doing as he was bid, Edward could not help the shame that crept up his cheeks as he sat with his leg stretched before him. What did she think of the man she had married? Was there a part of her that regretted his return? A part of her that wished he was dead after all?

"I do not know where to begin," she whispered, her blue eyes fixed on his face as she sat down opposite him, maintaining a careful distance between them. "I've dreamed of this moment, but I never thought..." Sighing, she shook her head.

Unbidden, Edward's heart rejoiced at her words, giving him false hope. "As have I," he replied, unable to silence himself.

A soft smile came to her face. "We're not the same anymore, are we? A lot has happened."

Edward nodded, forcing himself to speak, afraid of the painful silence that might descend upon them at any moment. "Ye did well... with the children." Carefully, he lifted his eyes and met her gaze. "They look well. They've grown strong and kind. Ye've been a great mother to them."

"I did my best," she replied, averting her gaze as though his praise bothered her. "But it hasn't always been easy."

Cringing under the hidden accusation Edward heard in her simple statement, he felt his hands clench. "I'm sorry for...leaving," he forced out through gritted teeth, his gaze fixed on the floor. "It wasn't right. I failed ye. I failed them. 'Twas foolish of me and selfish." Once again, his cheeks burnt with shame as he pushed himself to his feet. "I know

I don't deserve your forgiveness, and so I will not ask for it." Unable to look at her, Edward rushed from the room, feeling his throat close as the air was squeezed from his lungs. Not knowing where to turn, he hobbled out the front door and down the steps, welcoming the fresh air as it brushed over his heated face.

"Edward!"

At the sound of her voice, he stopped as though it held power over him, as though he could not leave without her permission. Listening to her approaching footsteps, he kept his gaze fixed on the horizon, for the thousandth time cursing himself for his foolishness in coming here. He ought to have known better.

As she stepped up to him, he could feel her closeness like a warm blanket, and his heart ached for her. "Will ye take a walk with me?" she asked, her gaze seeking his.

Swallowing, Edward nodded, unable to speak, and yet, unable to deny her. Would he stay if she asked? Or would he be able to resist her? Edward doubted it very much.

Slowly, they made their way down the small slope and past the manor house toward the tree line where Matthew had found his new favourite tree only a short while ago. Yet, it seemed like a small eternity had passed since then.

As they walked, Edward could feel her presence beside him. And within him, he felt all the old instincts reawaken. Never had he thought about how to speak to her, how to touch her. Always had his mind and heart and body acted as though they simply knew how they fit together.

And yet, he was no longer the man he used to be. Although he felt the urge to hold out his hand to her and aid her up the small slope-not because she could not do it herself, but simply because-Edward could not. For the moment he leaned toward her, his own balance became unhinged, and he almost lost his step, leaning heavily on the cane.

Gritting his teeth, he kept his gaze fixed straight ahead, doing his utmost to ignore the watchful look in her eyes. She did pity him. How could she not? All he had now was a pitiable existence. One not worth living.

"There," his wife said, and his head snapped up, his gaze following her hand gesturing to the small dip in the land where a group of men worked on a small cottage. The sound of hammering and sawing filled the still air, and the occasional chatter and laughter echoed to his ear. "'Tis our new home," she told him, pride ringing in her voice. "We'll be able to move in within a matter of days."

Grateful for the change of topic, Edward drew in a shaky breath as he stood beside her, watchful not to have his arm brush hers as he shifted his weight from one foot onto the other. "'Tis beautiful," he commented, remembering his son mentioning a storm, which had upended his favourite tree. "What happened to the old one?"

Meagan sighed, "Not long before Christmas last year, a heavy storm rolled in." Shaking her head, she inhaled deeply, her hands gripping her upper arms more tightly as she held them crossed before her chest. "I thought the world would end."

Edward swallowed, feeling unease crawl up his spine at the sight of her brave face. She had to have been terrified, and he had not been there to bear the burden with her.

"As solid and strong, even unyieldin', as that tree had always seemed," she continued, a touch of incredulity in her voice, "it snapped like kindling in the wind, destroying our home and trapping us inside."

Unaware of this part of the story, Edward sucked in a sharp breath, and his head whipped around as he stared at his wife. "The tree fell onto the cottage?"

Sighing, Meagan nodded before her eyes moved from the small home before them and turned to meet his. "We were, Erin and I, but Matthew found a way out. He went to the manor house for help." A deep smile came to her face, full of pride and awe. "And they came for us. All of them. I've never known such loyalty, and I shall never take it for granted."

Feeling his heart thud against his ribcage, Edward drew one deep breath after another into his lungs as a new sense of panic washed over him. Always had he thought his family safe from harm. Always had he thought he alone was the one in danger of losing his life.

Oh, what a fool he had been! Dangers lurked everywhere, and he had left his family alone to fend for themselves.

"Would it not be better to remain in the manor house?" Edward suggested, afraid of what might happen when the next storm hit. "Would that not be safer?"

Meagan shrugged. "Well, the tree cannot fall again, can it?"

"Still, there are all kinds of dangers that may befall ye," Edward objected, determined to make his point even though he knew he had no right to question her decisions. Not after abandoning her and forcing them on her in the first place. "I believe ye and the children would be safer at the manor."

As she inhaled deeply, slowly, Edward saw the muscles in her jaw tense before she slowly turned to face him. Her deep blue eyes held his, and he saw a spark of anger light up in them. "I want my own life," she said, her voice calm, and yet, her hands gripped her upper arms almost painfully. "I want my own home. I've fought for it all these years, and I shall not give it up."

Edward nodded, unable to lay further blame at her feet. "I understand. I did not mean to question ye. I have no right to. Ye did well all those years on your own. Ye were strong, and ye did what needed to be done."

Her lips thinned, and a hard stare came to her eyes. "I did not have a choice."

Again, Edward nodded, hearing the accusation of his failure in the tone of her voice, seeing it in the way she held his gaze. "I'm sorry for that. I'm sorry for puttin' all this on your shoulders. I had no right to, but I'm pleased to see that ye managed well. Ye're a strong woman, and ye've made a life for yourself here. I promise I shall not disrupt it."

Holding his gaze, she took a step closer, and her brows drew down slightly as a hint of confusion came to her eyes. "What are ye saying?"

Turning away like a coward, Edward swallowed. "I will leave on the morrow and not bother ye again."

Behind him, he heard her suck in a sharp breath. "Ye want to leave again? Why?"

Unable to answer her, Edward remained silent as the chaos in his heart and mind grew. Once he had been so certain of his course. Not anymore. With each minute he spent in her presence, uncertainty claimed him more and more as temptation reached out its hands to him. If he were to allow himself to see the truth that lived in his heart, he would realise that he wanted to stay. However, he did not dare, for he knew his duty above all else was to keep her safe, to keep them safe.

"Do ye not love me anymore?"

Her question felt like a stab to the heart, further weakening his resolve, and yet, Edward felt an undeniable pull. Like a siren, she called to him, and he knew he would not be able to resist her much longer. If he were to stay, he would pull her into his arms and never let her go again.

He could not risk that.

He had no right to risk her happiness ever again.

Pretending he had not heard her, Edward walked away, praying she would not stop him.

She did not.

Chapter Nine
THE NEED TO BE STRONG

Staring after her husband as he slowly made his way back toward the manor, Meagan felt an overwhelming need to sink into a puddle of misery and weep. Not since she had first received the news of her husband's death had she felt such a keen sense of loss, pain and desperation. Her heart ached as it already had once before, and she knew that a lot more pain lay ahead of her if he truly decided to leave.

Swallowing, Meagan gritted her teeth as they began to chatter, determination filling her being. She had survived his loss once, she could do so again.

Still, despite the utter sadness that overcame her, a small flame of anger ignited within her soul. After everything he had already put her through, how dare he do so again? Did he not know how close she had come to giving up? Could he not see that he was breaking her heart all over again? Or did he simply not care? Was this his way of telling her that he no longer loved her? His way of sparing her the pain of that knowledge?

Collecting what was left of her strength, Meagan slowly made her way toward the manor. Since her husband had entered from the front, she circled around toward the kitchen entrance, hearing her children's voices echo over from the yard. Unable to face them, she quickly ducked into the house, closing the door behind her.

As expected, Derek's mother Bessy stood at the workbench, her old, strong hands kneading dough, her eyes lifted in surprise as she took in Meagan's rattled state of mind. "Men are foolish creatures, are they not?"

Closing her eyes, Meagan nodded, feeling a single tear run down her cheek before she brushed it away. "He has no intention of stayin'," she whispered as though saying it out loud would make it true. "He wants to leave again." Walking over, Meagan sank onto one of the benches, leaning over and resting her arms and head on the tabletop. Inhaling deeply, she did her utmost to keep herself from losing her mind. How had this happened?

Not far from her, Bessy scoffed, and in her mind, Meagan could see the woman's disapproving scowl. "The war must've addled his brain. Did he tell ye why he wants to leave?"

Meagan sighed, then slowly lifted her head and met Bessy's kind eyes. "He did not. But from the way he spoke, I think he's afraid of failin' us again." She drew in a deep breath, remembering their conversation. "He had such a forlorn look in his eyes. I think he knows he acted foolish, and he feels ashamed."

Bessy nodded, her gaze softening. "I've seen such guilt before." Wiping her hands on her apron, she came to sit across from Meagan, gently placing her wrinkled hands on hers. "He feels out of place, my dear, out of place in his old life, and he does not know how to return to the man he once was. He's changed."

"I know that," Meagan replied, starting to feel annoyed. "As have I. I'm not the woman I used to be. I know he's been through hell, but," she swallowed as new tears threatened, "so have I. Can he not see that?"

Bessy shook her head, her hands gently squeezing Meagan's. "He cannot, dear. A part of him is still trapped on the battlefield, and he's afraid he will bring the war home with him. The world is not a happy place for him any longer, and he fears he will make ye lose sight of the beauties it holds." Her knowing eyes held Meagan's, imploring her. "Ye need to be strong now, dear."

Straightening her spine, Meagan almost yanked her hands out of Bessy's as she stared at the old woman, the muscles in her jaw clenching as indignation shot through her. "I've been strong for the past three years!" she snapped, fatigue clawing at her being. "I've raised two children on my own…with a broken heart no less. He never had to think of us as dead. He never had to find out what it meant to lose the one-" As sobs rose from her throat, Meagan broke off, burying her face in her hands.

Across from her, she heard Bessy rise to her feet and soon after felt the woman's comforting hands on her shoulders. "I know 'tis not fair," she said, compassion in her voice as she brushed her hands up and down Meagan's arms, "but the world has never been known to be so. He's made up his mind, and although the time may come when he will look back and regret his decision, it does not change how he feels right now."

Meagan sighed, closing her eyes. "I'm tired. I'm simply…tired."

"I know, dear," Bessy mumbled, wrapping her arms around Meagan's shoulders. "I know ye are, and ye have every right to be. But ye, too, will one day look back on the decision ye make now and come to regret it…if ye choose to let him walk out of your life now. Do ye truly wish for that? Or would ye rather take a stand now and avoid the regrets the future might hold?"

Deep down, Meagan knew that Bessy was right. If she allowed Edward to leave now, she would come to regret that decision for the rest of her life…every time she looked into her children's sad eyes. No, she needed to make him stay, and yet, she was not certain if she had the strength to do so.

"A blind man could see how much ye still love him," Bessy chuckled, "and he ye."

Meagan almost flinched at Bessy's words.

"Is that what ye're wonderin' about, dear?" the old woman asked. "If he still loves ye?"

"I cannot help but wonder," Meagan admitted. "If he did, would he truly consider leaving? Would it not break his heart to do so as it now breaks mine?"

For a long moment, Bessy remained quiet. Then she once more

stepped around the table and took the seat opposite Meagan. "I know losing someone ye love breaks your heart, but what's even worse is the fear of breaking theirs." A soft smile came to Bessy's face as she held Meagan's gaze. "What drives him is not a lack of love for ye, my dear. What drives him is the fear to hurt ye."

Inhaling deeply, Meagan stared at the old woman. "How do ye know this? Have ye even spoken a word to him since he arrived this mornin'?"

With a slight curl to her lips, Bessy shrugged. "Some things don't need words, dear. Some things are as plain to see as the sky overhead. Ye only need to know how to use your eyes." Then Bessy rose to her feet and returned to the dough on the workbench. "Don't let him slip through your fingers. The two of ye have been given a second chance that many can only dream of."

Hastening upstairs, Edward grabbed what few belongings he possessed and then made his way back down to the front hall. His gaze drifted from room to room as he approached the door. No one was around. No one was there to stop him. He could simply walk out the door and head down the lane. Keep walking until...

Until what? Where was he to go?

Instantly, an image of the cliff top rose before his inner eye, and although Edward knew it to be the right choice, he could not help but cringe at the thought of flinging himself into a wet grave.

"Are you truly such a coward," Derek's voice spoke from behind him, "to steal away without a word?"

Closing his eyes, Edward inhaled deeply, knowing he did not have the strength to face his friend's accusations once more. After all, they were justified.

"Talk to me, Edward," Derek demanded, coming to stand in front of him, his dark eyes calculating as he tried to understand what drove his best friend to such a decision. "Before you do anything rash, talk to me."

Lifting his head, Edward met his friend's gaze. "I've told ye what ye need to know. There's nothing else to say." He swallowed, opening his mouth once more before his courage could fail him. "Would ye look after them? Ensure their safety?"

For a long moment, Derek looked at him as though he could read his mind like a book. Always had he possessed such an unnerving ability to see behind lies and half-truths. "Don't pretend you're doing this for anyone but yourself," he said, his words painfully brutal; and yet, his voice full of compassion. "Whatever you've told me…or yourself is nothing but excuses. Your true reason for leaving, for running away, is simply that you're afraid." Placing a hand on Edward's shoulder, he held his gaze. "But fear is never a good reason to leave. It is never a good reason to do anything. If you let it, it will hold you trapped in its clutches for the rest of your life."

Sighing, Edward felt the pull of temptation strengthening. What his friend said was true. He was not so delusional to not be able to see that. And yet, his feet had been guided by an assumption that had kept him from losing his mind, from admitting the true depth of the guilt he felt. He knew he had failed his family, and the only way he now could handle that truth was by allowing himself to believe that they were better off without him.

Only now Derek's words began to chip away at the fortress he had built within himself, and Edward was terrified of the moment he would break through.

"You've made it back," Derek continued, without a doubt knowing exactly how his words affected his friend. "You've survived the war. Do not walk away from this last battle! For you're well-equipped to win it and be rewarded with a happy life, with a woman and two children who love you. The only question is, do you want them? Are you willing to fight for them?"

Gritting his teeth until the muscles in his jaw hurt, Edward did not dare allow himself to even contemplate these questions, for deep down, he knew that it would lead to his ruin.

Soft footsteps echoed to his ears from the direction of the kitchen, and his friend lifted his head, looking over Edward's shoulder.

Before Edward had even turned to look or heard her voice, he knew that it was Meagan. Even if he could not see her, somehow, he had always been able to sense her when she was near. It was as though her closeness changed the air around them, made it thicker, heavier, gentler. Almost like a caress. And his body strained toward her, knowing by instinct that it was there by her side where it belonged.

Only his mind forced his body to remain rooted to the spot, and his heart cursed him for it.

"Could ye give us a moment?" his wife spoke as she appeared in his peripheral vision.

Derek nodded. "Certainly." Then he walked away, leaving them alone.

Keeping his eyes fixed on the door and his mind on the decision he had made a long time ago, Edward tried his best to ignore the slight hum he felt in his bones, the soft tingle that came to his lips at the mere sight of her.

Taking a deep breath, Meagan turned to him. "I have some questions, and there are things I need ye to tell me. Ye owe me that."

Even out of the corner of his eye, he could see the tension on her face as she wrung her hands, trying to keep her wits about her.

"I would ask ye to stay until the morning—one night," she continued, her voice shaking. "If ye still wish to leave then," she swallowed, and her fingernails dug into her hands, "I will not stop ye."

Turning to look at her, Edward felt a stab of pain at the revelation that she would step back and allow him to leave. Still, he knew that he did not deserve anything more. "One night," he whispered, unable to deny her such a simple request.

Meagan nodded, tears glistening in her eyes. "One night. Ye have my word."

"All right," Edward finally said, unable not to do so, and yet, terrified of the desperate longing he felt growing in his heart with each moment spent in her presence.

A lot could happen in one night.

He could only hope he would be able to keep his wits about him.

However, he doubted it very much.

Chapter Ten
ONE NIGHT

After supper, Meagan entrusted the care of her children to the women of Huntington House, forcing her mind to focus on one thing alone: her husband.

When they had all sat down to eat that night, they had barely looked at one another over the rim of their bowls. Eyes cast downward, they had conversed with everyone else, but each other. It reminded Meagan of the first weeks after she had first lost her heart to him long ago. Then, too, they had barely looked at each other, seeking each other's presence but fearing to be alone just as much, uncertain of how the other felt, afraid to be disappointed.

Only now, the fear that lived in Meagan's heart was a thousand times worse. These were not the childish dreams of a young girl. No, what was at risk now was the life she had loved, the life she had thought lost before, and that loss had almost taken her will to live, to go on.

Would she be able to survive again?

With a small bag slung over one shoulder, Meagan led her husband through the tall grass toward her new cottage. A lantern held out before her allowed them to see the ground in front of them, and Meagan was careful to shine it before her husband's feet so that he would not stumble. Out of the corner of her eye, she could see the tension on his face as he carefully placed one foot in front of the other, afraid to lose his balance and fall.

He would be mortified. Meagan knew it to be true, and yet, she could not understand why. After all, was it not natural to have trouble walking after suffering such an injury? Why should anyone be ashamed of that? It was not his fault.

"The cottage is almost finished," she spoke into the night, trying to take their minds off the tension that hung in the air between them. "In a mere few days, we'll be able to move back in."

Barely glancing at her, Edward nodded his head, but did not respond. However, from the way his shoulders tensed, Meagan could tell that he did not approve. Did he truly think her incapable of caring for their children on her own? After all, anyone's house could have been destroyed in such a storm. It had not been her fault.

Opening the door, Meagan stepped inside the main room, the smell of fresh wood with a hint of sap touching her senses. Grateful that Derek and Sean had spent the afternoon setting up her furniture, she placed the lantern on the sturdy table by the kitchen workbench and unfastened her cloak, hanging it on a peg by the front door and placing her back by the far wall. Then she turned and found her husband standing by the side of the table, his eyes fixed on the small light, the look on his face forlorn.

"Here we are." Swallowing, Meagan forced herself not to drop her gaze. Who was this stranger who now stood across from her? A chill shot down her spine, and the muscles in her body tensed to prevent them from trembling. Would he guess her thoughts?

There were moments when she felt his presence as though he had his arms wrapped around her, his warmth filling her senses as that familiar cloud of love and devotion brushed over her skin. In these moments, it was as though no time had passed, and all she wanted to do was run into his embrace.

However, when she found herself meeting his eyes, the illusion was instantly stripped from her, and an unknown cold speaking of fear and apprehension reached out its claws for her. There was a darkness in him that had almost extinguished the light that had always shone in his eyes. It was as though the man she had once known did no longer exist. He had died on the battlefield, and the apparition before her was a soulless body.

A stranger.

Which was the truth?

Was there any chance for him to return to her? Or was all hope lost?

Looking at her husband, at his familiar face, from across the room, Meagan realised that although she wanted him back, she would not compromise. If he decided to stay, she would only accept him back if he truly *wanted* to...with all his heart and soul.

The alternative would break her heart, but at least it would be a quick break, not like a festering wound that would kill her a little more every day. No, she could not allow that to happen. She had her children to think of.

"Ye never intended to stay, did ye?" she finally asked, her voice feeble. Still, she did not blink, clenching her hands, willing more courage into her heart. Never had she cowered. She would not begin now. No matter how terrified she was.

Before he raised his gaze to hers, she could see the muscles in his jaw clench. Then he shook his head, the look in his eyes so full of sadness and pain that Meagan's heart ached for him.

"Then why did ye return?" she continued, welcoming the strength that surged through her body now that she was finally coming out of her hiding place and taking control.

Edward swallowed. "I needed to know that ye were safe."

"Are we?"

A slight frown came to his face as he held her gaze. Then he nodded.

Taking a step toward the table, Meagan noticed the slight narrowing of his eyes. "Ye should have known we would be. Did Derek not promise ye he would look after us?" Momentarily overwhelmed by the renewed thought of his loss, Meagan swallowed, pressing her lips together painfully to keep the tears at bay. "He's a good man. Ye knew he would never have broken his word."

Dropping his gaze, her husband shrugged.

"Then why did ye come?" Meagan demanded, relieved when the sorrow in her heart slowly subsided and her determination grew stronger. "After all, there was no need. Ye already knew what ye needed to."

Still, her husband remained quiet, uncomfortably shifting from one foot onto the other.

"Ye thought us married, did ye not?"

At her question, Edward's head snapped up and he stared at her, his gaze burning with things unsaid.

A smile tugged at the corners of Meagan's mouth, and she let it show, relieved to see him react in such a way. "Ye were jealous; is that not so?"

Instantly, he dropped his gaze, but the muscles in his jaw tensed to the point of breaking.

As he continued to avoid her, Meagan felt a small flame of anger ignite. How dare he? Had he not promised her one night? And answers? Did he truly think he was holding up his end of the bargain?

Gritting her teeth, she stepped closer, her eyes hard, unyielding. "Since ye do not intend to stay," she said, "I suppose it would not bother ye if I were to remarry."

For a moment, she thought he would double over as though someone had punched him in the stomach. A strangled moan rose from his throat, and Meagan felt her heart skip a beat. He did care, didn't he?

Then he lifted his head and met her eyes, his own dark and full of meaning. "Do as ye wish," he forced out through clenched teeth.

Disappointed, Meagan swallowed. "Would it bother ye?" she pressed, unwilling to let him sway her from her path. She wanted the truth. She needed the truth.

Pressing his lips together, Edward remained quiet, his gaze locked with hers, his nostrils flaring.

Hands on her hips, she snapped, "Would it?"

"Yes!" he growled, his left hand tightening on his cane.

"Why?"

Gritting his teeth, he shook his head as though to force his answer back down before it could fly from his lips.

"Why?" Meagan pressed, advancing on him. "Why?"

His eyes burnt into hers.

"Why?"

The muscles in his throat convulsed.

"Tell me!" Standing but an arm's length apart, she stared up at him, fierce determination urging her on. "Why?"

His body shook as his emotions ran rampant.

"Why?"

"Because ye're mine!" he snarled, the words flying from his lips before he had even made the decision to answer. She could see the shock of it on his face.

Swallowing, he dropped his gaze and took a step back as though ashamed.

Joy flooded Meagan's heart not only at the words he had spoken but also at the honest emotion that had accompanied them. "Do ye still love me?" she whispered, her gaze softening as she looked at his pale face.

Slowly, he raised his eyes to hers, shock still resting on his features.

"Please, tell me," she urged him gently. "Do ye still love me?"

After drawing in a slow breath, he swallowed. "Heaven help me, but I do."

Staring at his wife, Edward felt his body begin to tremble with the effort it took him to keep her at arm's length. She stood so close that he could simply reach out and...

But he must not. It would not be right. It would not be good for her. Not in the long run.

Still, the way she had just attacked him and demanded an answer had only served to remind him of the fire she had always possessed. The fire he had always admired. The fire that had drawn him to her side from the very beginning.

And he still loved her the way he always had.

There was no denying that.

And that knowledge lit up her eyes and painted one of the most beautiful smiles on her face he had ever seen. Edward could have looked at her forever. If only she would have let him.

But, of course, she did not.

Slowly, the relieved joy that had come to her face at his words subsided, once more replaced by the fierce determination she had attacked him with before. Of course, she was not done. Far from it. She would strip him bare and steal all his secrets before the sun rose the next morning.

Cursing himself, Edward drew in a slow breath. He should never have agreed to this. It had been foolish of him.

"If ye do," she asked, the tone in her voice gentle despite the fierceness that burned in her eyes, "then why do ye intend to leave?"

Edward sighed, knowing that he owed her the truth. "To protect ye," he forced out through gritted teeth, for although he had told himself so countless times, it was a different matter to say it out loud... and to her of all people. "I'm no longer the man I used to be. I'm no longer good for ye." Holding her gaze, he willed her to understand... and to let him go. "I've changed, deep inside, in a way that..." He shook his head. "I no longer fit into this life. The world around me is dark and cold, and I do not wish ye to be affected by that. Ye deserve better. Ye deserve what I can no longer give ye."

Nodding, she drew in a deep breath. "I hear what ye're saying, and I can see the truth of it in your eyes, but I do not agree that all hope is lost."

Holding his gaze, she took a step closer, and Edward almost shrank back, his eyes wide as he stared at her.

"Your world is cold and dark because ye allow it to be so," she counselled, her blue eyes dark in the dim light. "Ye've nothing to live for, no one to chase away the darkness and warm your heart. Do not push me away for I can help ye." Reaching out a hand, she placed it on his upper arm. "Please, let me help ye."

Edward sucked in a sharp breath as he felt her touch through the layers of his clothing, and his skin tingled with the memory of what it felt like with no barrier between them.

As his heart yearned for her with a passion long since ignored, panic seized him, and he jerked back, severing the connection between them. "Ye're not to help me!" he growled, shaking his head. "I am your husband, and 'tis my duty to come to *your* aid, to see *ye* safe, to protect *ye*." As the words left his lips, Edward knew them to be a mistake.

Although clearly disappointed before, Meagan's eyes now narrowed, once more burning with righteous anger as she stepped toward him. "Do not speak to me thus!" she snapped, pointing an accusing finger at him. "Everyone is weak sometimes, and everyone can be strong." She swallowed, tears brimming in her eyes, and yet, the fire that burnt within her would not allow her to back down. "When ye left, it changed my life. Suddenly, I was responsible for everything all by myself, and I did what I could because I had to." She drew in a steadying breath. "Over time, though, I came to realise something: my own strength. It gave me a new insight into my own abilities, and I'm grateful for it."

Watching her, Edward could see what his rash decision had done to her. Still, she had persevered and was stronger for it. He was certain she could do so again.

"Why do ye think I wish for ye to stay?" she demanded, catching him off guard with her question. "To fix the house? To chop wood?" She shook her head. "I don't need ye for that. I can do all that by myself, and should I find myself in need of assistance, I have people in my life who will stand with me...no matter what."

Edward's shoulders slumped, and all blood drained from his face. Although she had just told him what he had wanted her to understand, to come to realise, her words still knocked the air from his lungs. She did not need him.

Inhaling deeply, she took another step closer, her gaze seeking his. "I don't need ye to stay," she whispered, and his heart broke into a thousand little pieces, "not for that." Her hands reached for him, slowly running up his arms, as her eyes held his.

Edward swallowed, thoroughly confused as his body warmed under her touch.

"I don't *need* ye to stay," she repeated as her hands came to rest on his shoulders. "But I *want* ye to stay."

Staring at her, Edward felt a frown drawing down his brows.

Seeing his confusion, his wife rolled her eyes, then grabbed him by the collar and yanked him against her, almost upending his balance. "What a daft fool ye are, Edward Dunning! Can ye not see that I love ye as well? That I've always loved ye and always will?" Her jaw clenched as she glared at him. "And I'll be damned if I allow ye to break my heart all over again."

Chapter Eleven
THE REASON WITHIN

Seeing her husband stare at her, dumbfounded at her words as though he had truly believed her love for him gone for good, Meagan detected a faint glimmer of the man she had once known. In shock, his guard had fallen away, and the eyes that held hers shone with the same hope and dreams as they had long ago. His body relaxed, and she could feel his chest rise and fall with each breath. His gaze held hers for a long time, and then-as he had done countless times in another life-his arms came around her, pulling her closer.

Meagan sighed at the feel of his embrace, so shockingly familiar that it stole the breath from her throat. How often had she grasped at this feeling in her dreams? Only to have it fall short of the reality of her husband's touch, knowing that the memory alone would never be enough?

"Meagan," he whispered a moment before his cane clattered to the floor and his arms pulled her hard against him. Then his mouth claimed hers with a desperate fierceness she knew only too well, wiping away three years of separation.

Three years without the other's touch.

Three years without the magic of those three little words.

It had been too long.

Crushed in his embrace, Meagan allowed herself to live in the moment. Abandoning all fears and doubts, she returned his kiss, reacquainting herself with her husband's touch, the taste of his lips, the feel of his body.

He, too, seemed driven as though mad, fiercely clutching her to him as though she might disappear if he loosened his hold on her for the barest of moments. His lips devoured hers, reclaimed her as his. *Because ye're mine!* He had growled, and she could only hope he meant it.

But he did not.

The moment her arms encircled his neck, tightening her hold on him, he broke the kiss, staring down at her as though he did not recognise her. Swallowing, he released her, stumbling backwards, almost losing his footing.

Meagan's heart began to ache anew, and she cursed herself for entertaining such foolish hope. Still, she could not walk away even if it meant risking her heart all over again.

"I apologise," her husband stammered, his gaze not meeting hers, but glancing around the floor until it fell on the cane. Then he bent down awkwardly, his face contorted and his cheeks flushing red, to pick it up. As he straightened, he took another step back, away from her. "I'm not the man I used to be," he mumbled, unable to meet her eyes, but instead glancing at the door.

Did he truly intend to run from her? Kiss her and leave?

"No matter what we say," he continued, glancing down at his injured leg, "nothing can change what happened. No good can come from pretending that I am still the man ye once knew. I'll only hurt ye, and I've already done so. I could not live with myself if I did so again."

Fortifying herself with another deep breath, Meagan stood up straight, her eyes seeking his, unwilling to allow him to escape. "And ye don't think that I have changed? That everything that has happened in the past years has made me a woman different from the one ye knew?"

Carefully meeting her gaze, Edward swallowed, indecision and a fair amount of temptation clear in his eyes.

Encouraged, Meagan forged on. "We've all changed. We cannot undo that, but maybe we don't need to. People change all the time. As life moves, so do we."

Shaking his head, her husband glanced down at his leg. "That is not the same. I haven't merely changed. I've become a burden. Ye would not want...that."

Watching him, Meagan wondered about the slight hesitation as he spoke. Had he truly meant to say what he had? Or had he meant to say that she would not want *him*? Did he doubt her love for him? Did he truly believe that a mere injury could ever dissuade it?

With her hands on her hips, ready to attack his reasoning with everything she had, Meagan stepped toward him. "Tell me this, would it bother ye if I had a leg like yours?" His head snapped up, his eyes wide as they met hers. "Would ye no longer want me? Love me?"

His mouth opened as though he was about to answer, but then reconsidered. His gaze narrowed, and a touch of suspicion came to his eyes as though he had just realised the reason behind her questions and refused to take the bait. "It would not be the same."

Annoyed, Meagan crossed her arms before her chest. "Ye keep saying that. Still, it makes as little sense as it did the first time ye did."

Gritting his teeth, he took a step toward her, his gaze holding hers; and in that moment, Meagan knew without the shadow of a doubt that they were nearing the true reason for the tortured look in his eyes. "Because mine is a punishment," he growled, disgust clear in his voice as he glanced down at the offending limb.

"Punishment?" Meagan frowned. "What do ye mean?"

Sighing, he chose his words. "I did not simply mean my leg, but everything that happened since the day I left."

Although Meagan could see that the words he spoke pained him, there was also a touch of relief in his gaze as though he felt liberated to be able to speak his mind after such a long time.

"I was injured," he continued, his gaze distant, seeing images of the past, "and then left for dead." He blinked, and his gaze met hers once more. "I was declared dead. For all intents and purposes, I was."

"It was a mistake," Meagan objected, feeling goose bumps crawl up her arms at the resigned tone in her husband's voice.

"Was it?" he demanded. "Or was it a sign?"

"A sign for what?"

He licked his lips and swallowed as though seeking to prolong the inevitable. "That I was meant to die." Again, he swallowed, and regret filled his eyes. "Maybe the world would be a better place without me. Maybe I should have died on that field."

Staring at her husband, Meagan felt a cold shiver grab her body as she realised the depth of his torment. "How can ye think that?" Taking a deep breath, she placed a gentle hand on his arm, ignoring the way his muscles jerked as though trying to put some distance between them. "And even if ye think it a sign, why do ye believe ye were meant to die? Maybe ye were meant to live. Ye survived the impossible. Is that not even more reason to believe into a second chance?"

"I wish I could," he whispered, an almost desperate need to believe her in his voice. "But I know I do not deserve it." As his lips pressed into a thin line, he nodded his head. "'Tis a punishment. A well-deserved one."

"A punishment for what? What did ye do that would justify such a punishment?"

Lifting his gaze, he met her eyes, his own narrowed in confusion. "Why would ye ask me this? You of all people know."

Sighing in exasperation, Meagan felt her gaze harden. "Would ye quit speaking in riddles? If ye haven't noticed, today has been…a day like no other. I do not care for this guessing game. Now, tell me, what ye believe this punishment to be for."

"For leaving ye!" he snapped back at her, his eyes closing as the full weight of his words sank in. "For not appreciating what I had. For recklessly risking my family, my home, my life…with ye and the children." Swallowing, he opened his eyes and met hers. "And for what? For the distant notion of glory and adventure? Today, I cannot believe the fool I have been. And yet, it does not change what was, what I did. I sacrificed ye, and now I have no right to reclaim ye." As his gaze searched her face, his brows drew down. "Are ye not angry at me for that?"

※ ❀ ※

Watching the emotions play over her beautiful face-from determination to annoyance to utter shock-Edward could barely keep his wits about him. His body hummed with her closeness as his eyes traced the gentle curve of her neck, the line of her lips and lingered on the blazing fire in her ocean blue gaze. Her golden curls were in disarray, and her cheeks slightly flushed, and his fingers yearned to feel her skin against his own once more.

He should never have come. Never had he been able to resist her. She was the embodiment of all his hopes and dreams. She had always been. And despite everything that had changed, that was the one thing that had remained constant.

"Yes, I am angry with ye."

Jerked out of his musings, Edward stared at her, his heart aching from the sting of her words. Swallowing, he nodded, "Ye've every right to-"

"Let me finish!" she interrupted, the look in her eyes dangerous as she stepped toward him, her right hand lifted in accusation as she jabbed a finger into his chest again and again, emphasising the anger she spoke of. "Ye left us, and, yes, I was angry with ye. Maybe I still am. What ye did was foolish and rash, the actions of a dreamer." She sighed. "And yet, I let ye go. Some mistakes need to be made. Some things cannot be learnt from another's experience. Some things have to be felt and suffered and endured." She swallowed, and her eyes softened as her fingers curled into the front of his shirt. "Ye needed to know, or ye would have been forever left wondering. 'Twasn't your fault for wanting...more. The heart wants what it wants. Do ye blame me for letting ye go? For not fighting for ye to stay?"

Yet again, Edward found himself staring at his wife, at the kindness and compassion in her eyes. He heard honest understanding and utter willingness to forgive and forget in her voice, and he felt the lightness of her touch, gentle and yet demanding. And he knew beyond the shadow of a doubt what she was offering.

"Stay," she whispered, a quiet plea, as her eyes filled with tears. "We are a family. That never changed. Ye're the father of my children. Ye're my husband." She inhaled deeply, and her body moved into his, pulling him closer against her. "I want ye back."

Traitorously, the muscles in his arms itched with the need to reach for her, to accept what she offered and ignore the weight of his conscience. Her lips beckoned him into a kiss, and her words brought back memories of happier times.

Feeling his defences crumble into dust, Edward took a step back and his hands removed her hold on him. He did not dare look at her, meet her eyes, for he knew it would break his heart. Although he wanted her as much as ever before, he could not give in.

Not now.

Not again.

"If ye don't wish to stay," Meagan asked, her voice choked with tears, "then where will ye go?"

Edward swallowed. He could not tell her.

"Will ye find a new home in another village and start anew? Will ye live a separate life away from us?" With each word, anger returned to her voice. "Will ye start a new family?"

Unwilling to leave her in the agony of her suspicions, Edward swallowed, "I do not mean to live anywhere." He dropped his gaze and stepped around her. "I told ye I was meant to die on the continent. That has not changed."

For a long moment, everything remained quiet, and Edward did not dare turn around to look at her.

Then he heard the rustle of her skirts, and a second later, she stepped in front of him, her eyes round, searching his face. "Do ye truly mean to kill yourself?"

Edward drew in a slow breath.

Fresh tears brimmed in her eyes, but she blinked them away. "If that was your intention, why did ye come? Why did ye not take your own life before coming back here? Before revealing yourself to us?" An angry snarl came to her lips. "Why did ye come?"

Gritting his teeth, Edward felt his grip on his cane tightening. "I told ye why I came," he snapped, inhaling the fresh scent of her soft skin...so close. Too close. "I would ask that ye stop trying to persuade me to stay. I've made up my mind and I will not-"

"How dare ye!"

Meeting her gaze, her eyes wild and unwavering, Edward felt his hands clench as he struggled with the contrasting emotions surging through him. "For once, I want to do what is best, what is reasonable, what is responsible. If I follow my heart, it will only lead me to ruin as it has before. I must do what is right, not what I want."

"What ye want?" his wife whispered, the look on her face not one of anger any longer. "What is it that ye want? What lives in your heart?"

Realising his mistake, Edward tried to back away. "I should leave."

"But that is not what ye want, is it?" Meagan demanded, the look in her eyes saying that she knew well the temptation he was battling. Holding his gaze, she placed her hands on his chest once more, and a soft smile curled up her lips at his sudden intake of air. "What ye want is what I want as well."

Fear gripped Edward's heart. "But-"

"Ye owe me one night," she whispered, her lips brushing against his ever so slightly.

Taken aback, Edward almost lost his footing as his cane clattered to the floor for the second time that night. Instantly, his arms came around her, holding her closer. For balance, he told himself, and yet, deep down, he knew it to be a lie.

Inhaling deeply, her eyes sobered. "Ye're free to choose," she told him, her voice heavy with regret. "I will not take that from ye. No matter what happens between us tonight, if ye wish to leave in the mornin', I will not stop ye...even though it'll break my heart all over again."

Edward felt his own eyes fill with tears as he looked down at her, her body resting gently against his. They fit together. They always had.

"I want one night." Lifting her head, she met his eyes, and her arms came around his neck. "I demand it. Ye owe me a night free of the past and the future, free of doubt and regret. I've dreamt of ye so often, and now ye're here. Right here in my arms." Tears spilled over as she smiled at him. "And now, I cannot let ye go without feeling your touch once more. I've dreamt of it countless times, and it was never enough."

Edward swallowed, knowing exactly what she meant.

Feeling his resolve waver and then disappear, he tightened his hold on her, noting the relieved curl of her lips as she pulled him down to her. Then her mouth claimed his, and the chains of the past fell from him. Time lost all meaning as her warmth surrounded him, gently putting his mind at ease and soothing the ache in his bones.

Sometime in the night, Edward caught a glimpse of the man he once had been.

A man he had thought lost long ago.

And for a moment, he could not remember a single reason why on earth he would leave his wife.

Was it madness?

Chapter Twelve
AT A CROSSROAD

S till lost in her dreams, Meagan smiled, delighted with the details her senses had conjured for her. Never had her husband seemed as real to her as he had that night. It was almost as though her hand truly rested on his chest, feeling the warmth of his skin and the soft rise and fall of his breathing.

Snuggling closer, Meagan wished she could remain in this dream world for good. However, the moment that thought occurred, she remembered that she had thought so once before, and she had almost lost herself in those dreams.

Empty dreams.

Memories of a life lost forever.

Still, she could feel him as though he were right here with her. If she opened her eyes though, she knew she would find the other side of the bed empty…as it always had been.

The echo of children's laughter drifted to her ears, and she frowned, feeling the soft lull of slumber pull away. More sounds reached her mind. Birds chirped in the distance, their song almost drowned out by the strong wind that blew around the cottage.

Don't wake up! Her soul screamed at her.

But there was nothing she could do.

Inevitably, her dreams would vanish in the light of day, bringing back a harsh reality she wished she could forget.

Sighing, Meagan opened her eyes...to find her husband sleeping beside her, his left hand covering hers as it rested on his chest.

Frozen, all Meagan could do was stare before her heart reawakened and a sudden joy surged to the surface, warming her chilled limbs and returning the memories of the previous night.

"It wasn't a dream," Meagan whispered, tears rolling down her cheeks as she looked down at Edward's sleeping form. "He's here. He's truly here."

Overwhelmed, Meagan felt the desperate need to fling herself into his arms, to wake him and hear him say that it was true, that he was not dead, that he had retur-

But he had not, had he?

As more pieces of the previous night fell into place, Meagan felt an icy cold spread through her limbs. Had she truly told him she would let him go? How could she have been so foolish? One night was not enough, not nearly enough.

After getting him back so unexpectedly, she could not simply allow him to walk out of her life again. She could not! No matter what she had to do, she could not allow him to leave. If need be, she would tie him to the bed and-

Sighing, Meagan closed her eyes.

She could not. As much as she wanted to, she could not.

Not because she had given him her word, but because it was *his* choice.

It had to be.

If she made it for him, he would never truly *be* here. His body, yes; but his heart and soul would continue to struggle.

No, this was a decision he would have to make for himself.

What if he decides to leave?

Gritting her teeth, Meagan swallowed. "Then I will let him go."

With tears streaming down her face, she slid from the bed. As she reached for her clothes, Meagan heard him stir behind her and turned to find him brushing a hand over his face. Then his eyes found hers, and they held the same incredulity she herself had experienced a moment earlier.

"When I woke up, I thought I was still dreaming," she whispered, a soft smile on her face. "I couldn't believe ye were truly here."

Swallowing, he nodded, and she could see the memories of the previous night returning. Would he hold her to her word?

Quickly, Meagan turned her back to him and hastily pulled on her clothes. Then she rushed from the bedroom and back to the main room where she leaned heavily on the backrest of a chair and buried her face in her hands. "Stay calm," she whispered to herself as her heart hammered in her chest. "Ye have to do this. Somehow ye have to find the strength to do this."

"Are ye all right?" came her husband's voice from the bedroom door. Then she heard him walk toward her, dragging his left leg awkwardly.

Even without turning to look at him, Meagan could picture the contorted expression of his face, the slight blush that reddened his cheeks as he bent down to pick up the cane he had dropped the night before. He felt broken. She knew that. Not worthy of her love.

It was a ludicrous thought, and yet, she did not know how to convince him that, for her, nothing had changed. He was as whole as he had always been.

Unfortunately, he would have to realise that for himself, and she was not certain if he ever would.

As Meagan turned to him, her gaze brushed over the small carving knife one of her neighbours often used for whittling small figurines for his sons and daughters. He had to have forgotten it the day before when they had still worked on readying her cottage.

"Are ye all right?" Edward asked again, now leaning heavily on his cane as though he could not stand without it.

Meagan nodded, then drew back her shoulders and lifted her head. *Now or never*, she told herself. "Ye need to make a choice," she said, willing her voice not to break.

Her husband's gaze narrowed as though he had rather avoid that topic as well.

Forcing herself to continue down the path she had chosen, Meagan reached for the small carving knife. "I need ye to know," she began as her eyes held his, "that I love ye as I always have and that the thought of us being a family again is a dream come true."

The muscles in his jaw quivered, and for a moment, he dropped his gaze, inhaling deeply.

"I want ye to stay, but if ye cannot, if ye truly wish to leave and take your own life," she forced out, feeling tears stream down her face, "then ye might as well do it now."

Instantly, his head snapped up, and he stared at her before his gaze travelled down to the knife in her hands.

Swallowing, Meagan gently placed the small blade on the table beside her and then approached her husband.

For an eternal moment, they looked at each other. Then she gently cupped a hand to the side of his face. "I love ye, Edward. Never doubt that." Pulling him down to her once more, she placed a gentle kiss on his lips before stepping back. "Goodbye," she whispered, then turned and almost bolted for the door.

As the door closed behind her, Edward felt as though he had strayed into a nightmare.

Is this not what ye wanted?

Gritting his teeth, Edward swallowed. She was letting him go. More than that. If it was truly his choice, then she would not even try to-

Again, he swallowed, remembering the tears that had streamed down her face, the anguish in her eyes as she had bid him farewell and the slight tremble in her limbs as she had forced herself out the door.

She had done it for him.

For if it were up to her, they would never part ways again.

Images of happier days floated into Edward's mind, and he could not help the soft smile that came to his lips from growing ever bigger and wider, filling his heart with emotions he had long since thought lost. Was there truly a chance for him to return?

Had he not *already* returned?

Closing his eyes, Edward remembered the previous night in his wife's arms, their passionate encounter as they had slowly step by step rediscovered one another. Although she had changed-clearly-she was still the same woman he had fallen in love with. She could still see into his heart. She could still set his blood on fire with a single look.

She still loved him as she always had…did she not?

Even if he had thought it impossible, it had proven real and true.

Glancing around the cottage, Edward could picture a future there… with his wife and his children. He knew he ought not to. He was being selfish, and yet, he could not help himself. More than anything, he wanted to come home.

"Home," he whispered, remembering the many cold and lonely days of the past three years. Only now they were of the past, and what lay ahead of him was warm and welcoming and full of love.

If only he had the courage to claim it.

Sighing, Edward's gaze drifted down to the small craving knife Meagan had left for him. If their roles had been reversed, he would never have had the strength to allow her to make her own decision. He would have tied her to the bed to keep her from leaving, from hurting herself.

"She truly loves me," he whispered, hearing the same awe in his voice that he felt in his heart. Once again, he looked down at his leg, useless and awkward, and suddenly, he understood that she did not care. Did not mind.

His wife still loved him.

Turning away from the table and the knife upon it, Edward walked toward the door, his hand resting on the handle as he hesitated, old doubts stilling his movements.

Still, as the sun streamed in through the window, bathing the interior of the cottage in a warm glow, Edward could not remain where he was. Meagan was right. If he wanted to leave, he might as well end his life here and now.

But he could not.

More than that.

He did not want to.

There was too much to live for.

As the last of his shackles fell from him, Edward pulled open the door and stepped outside into a new day. In the distance, up on a small slope, he caught sight of his wife as she stood in the strong wind, her hair and skirts blown about, making her look so...alive.

Selfish or not, he could not give her up.

She was his...as he was hers.

The way it had always been.

In that moment, a blood-curdling scream broke the peaceful scene, and Edward was flung back through time, his mind dragging him to the terror and panic of the battlefield. Instantly, his body tensed, and he ducked low, his leg stretched out beside him, his cane lying useless by his side.

"Mummy! Help!"

Erin?

As his head jerked up, Edward caught sight of his wife running like a madwoman down the small slope toward a cluster of trees. Even from a distance, he could see the terror on her face, and his heart twisted in agony.

For a moment, Edward remained frozen to the spot before an old fire ignited within, and he pushed himself back onto his feet. Letting his gaze fly over the scene before him, he spotted his daughter, -his little girl, -high up in Matthew's new tree, her little hands wrapped around a branch, her feet dangling in the air.

Edward almost doubled over at the sight, fear surging through his body.

Then a single thought entered his mind, and everything else ceased to matter.

I cannot lose her!

Chapter Thirteen
TO FALL & RISE

Despite the warmth of the sun on her back, Meagan's limbs were ice-cold as she raced down the small slope between her new cottage and the manor house, her gaze fixed on the tall fir tree in the distance.

Too far! Her mind screamed, as her eyes held on to the small girl dangling in the air. *It's too far! Ye'll never make it!*

Fear gripped Meagan's heart at the realisation. Even from a distance, she could see Erin fight to keep her grip upon the branch, her small face distorted with effort and terror. She would not be able to hold on much longer.

Then something moved near the tree, and Meagan could not help but feel proud as she saw her son climb the tree after his sister, his long arms and legs pushing him upward with precision and care. He had truly grown up!

Still, would he be able to pull her up? Would she not drag them both down?

Meagan's stomach lurched at the thought, and she doubled her efforts, her feet flying over the ground as fast as her legs could take her.

"Erin!"

Her husband's voice cut through the haze of Meagan's terror, and her head jerked around.

After being on her own for the past three years, Meagan had completely forgotten Edward's return, his presence in their lives once more. But would he stay?

Staring at him as he stood just outside the cottage, his gaze wide open in horror as he stared at their daughter, Meagan willed him to move. Closer to the tree and their children by at least half, Edward still stood a chance to reach them in time. But could he? What about his leg? His cane? Could he even-?

The moment her husband flung himself forward, running awkwardly with his left leg held sideways toward the cluster of trees, his cane forgotten on the ground, Meagan felt tears come to her eyes.

"Hold on, Erin!" he yelled, pushing himself to run faster. "I'm coming!"

Meagan's heart rejoiced at seeing him like this as it proved once and for all-despite his objections-that he was still the man she had married long ago. He was still the man he had always been. He might have made a mistake, taken a wrong turn; however, few people could claim to be free of error. What mattered was that he had found his way back and that he loved her...them.

When Edward finally reached the tree, Meagan breathed a sigh of relief. Still, she kept running, her gaze fixed on her husband as he started up the tall fir tree, doing his best to accommodate his stiff leg. Here and there, he slipped or could not swing his left leg over a branch to pull himself up as it would not curl around the branch to hold him. However, he kept going.

Up and up, he went.

And Meagan knew that today was truly a new beginning.

If only they could save their daughter.

With terror in his heart, Edward made his way up the tree, sweat streaming down his face as the rough bark cut into his hands. Still, all he could do was stare at the little girl-his little girl!-dangling with her feet in the air, her eyes wide with the same terror he felt pulsing in his own veins.

What if she fell? What if he lost her? Was there a fate worse than losing one's child?

Gritting his teeth, Edward pushed on, ignoring the doubts that ate at his heart. He might not be the man he once had been, but he was Erin's father. It was his duty to save her. To protect her. To keep her safe.

For the rest of her life.

And it would not end today. Not today!

As Edward willed his body to obey his commands, a distant part of him realised how foolish he had acted, how foolish his reasoning had been. How could he have ever considered leaving his family again? How could he have been so blind?

Again, Erin's scream pierced the stillness of the day, and Edward's heart froze as his head jerked up, half-expecting to see her falling, picturing her broken body lying on the ground.

Bile rose in his throat, but Edward ignored it, focusing on the relief he felt when he found her little hands still curled around the branch.

"Hold on, Erin!" Matthew called, sitting on a branch beside the one carrying Erin's weight. Occasionally, he would lean over, reaching for his sister's arm, but the look on his face told Edward that he doubted he would be able to pull her up. If she released her grip and held on to him, they would both fall. "Father's coming for ye! He's almost there! He will save ye!"

As his son's voice echoed in his head, Edward could not believe the unadulterated trust and conviction he heard. After everything that had happened, after he had left his family and been absent for three years-almost all their lives-his son still believed in him.

More than ever before, Edward knew he could not disappoint his children. They depended on him because he was their father, and he would not fail them.

Cursing his leg, Edward pulled himself up yet another branch when Erin's little voice, full of panic, called out to him. The sound pierced his heart, and he realised how much he had missed them.

How much he had missed being a father.

Being their father.

Holding on to a thick branch, Edward swung his stiff leg forward until the hollow between heel and leg came to rest on the next higher branch. Then he pushed himself upward, his leg sliding over the branch more and more until he was able to right himself. Panting under his breath, he lifted his head and found his daughter just above him. If he stood, he might be able to reach her.

Slowly, Edward began pushing himself to his feet before he stopped and quickly removed his boots, throwing them to the ground. With his bare feet, it was easier by far to keep his balance, and holding on to the trunk with one hand, he stood up, bending himself left and right around smaller branches barring his way.

Then he lifted his head...and her little toes touched his nose.

Startled for a moment, Edward reached out...just as Erin's fingers slipped from the branch.

A shriek escaped her lips as she plummeted down, smaller branches scratching her arms and legs as well as her cheeks, and she pinched her eyes shut.

Feeling rather than seeing her fall, Edward acted on instinct.

As his body detected the light weight sliding past him, his arms shot out, releasing their secure hold, and reflexively grasped for the small child. Swaying on his feet, Edward felt his toes curl around the branch to maintain his balance as his arms tightened on his little daughter hanging awkwardly in his arms. Her hands curled into his shirt, pinching his skin, and she held on, burying her face against his shoulder.

Shifting his weight to rest against the trunk, Edward closed his eyes and breathed a sigh of relief, his arms holding his precious daughter.

Safe.

She was safe.

For a long moment, Edward simply stood there, hearing her sob, feeling her little heart beat against his chest, and cherished the moment.

She was alive.

"Father, ye did it!" Matthew cheered, swinging himself easily from branch to branch and coming to sit on one near his father and sister. "I thought she'd fall, but ye caught her!"

Smiling at his son, Edward nodded, unable to find words…any words. Too overwhelmed, all he could do was smile with relief, and joy, and utter delight.

"Are ye all right?"

Startled, Edward jerked his head to the side and glanced down, finding his wife halfway up the tree as she made her way toward them, relief clear on her face. Before long, she settled on a nearby branch, her hand reaching out to squeeze his.

Swallowing, Edward nodded. "We're fine," he whispered, unable to look anywhere else but into her dark blue eyes…so full of life and promise.

Lifting her little head, Erin glanced up at him, a shy smile playing on her lips. Then she turned and craned her neck. "Mummy?"

"I'm here, sweetheart," Meagan said, holding out her arms to receive her daughter.

Reluctantly, Edward released her, knowing that he could not claim an equal place in Erin's heart as Meagan. At least not yet.

He would have to earn her trust and her love and prove to her every day that he was here…and that he would not leave.

"Mother, did ye see that?" Matthew asked eagerly, exuberance bubbling under his skin. "Father truly is a hero, is he not?"

Taken aback by his son's words, Edward stared at his wife, who nodded her head, a mischievous smile slowly curling up the corners of her lips as she held his gaze. "I've always known him to be," she said then, her eyes fixed on Edward. "Only for a moment he was the one to forget." She drew in a deep breath, all tension falling from her. "But I think he is startin' to remember."

Sighing, Edward nodded. "I am," he whispered, not wanting his children to know that he had ever thought about leaving them. "Thank ye for remindin' me."

"Ye're welcome," Meagan said, reaching out and squeezing his hand. "And don't ye ever forget again."

Edward shook his head. "I'd be a fool to do so."

For a long while, they sat up in the tree, the promise of a new beginning hanging in the fresh morning air and simply enjoyed the moment.

A simple moment.

And yet, life-altering.

Then, down below by the base of the tree, someone cleared his throat, and they all looked down.

Barely able to hide a grin, Derek stood there, a mischievous twinkle in his eyes. "What are you all doing sitting in the tree?"

Meagan laughed, "Enjoying the view."

Chuckling, Derek shook his head, "You might want to come down to breakfast before Kara's finished it all. Remember, she's eating for two...at least."

Matthew giggled, and even Erin seemed inclined to ignore the turbulent events of that morning and head inside to fill her belly.

Slowly, they made their way down the tree, each taking turns to climb down a little and handing Erin to the other. Naturally, Matthew was the first to get his feet back on the ground and waited rather impatiently for the rest of his family. "Collin will be dyin' to hear what happened!" he beamed, grabbing Erin's little hand and pulling her onward to the manor house, following in Derek's wake.

Reaching for Meagan's hand, Edward pulled her back, his gaze finding hers. "I knew even before...," he glanced up the tree, "...that I could not leave. I think I've known the moment I laid eyes on ye again."

"Ye hid it well," Meagan said, smiling. Still, Edward could see the strain of the past day on her face. Had it only been one day? It seemed like a lifetime had passed since he had first set foot in Huntington House.

"I'm sorry," he whispered, cursing himself for putting her through such heartache. "I shall never leave ye again. Not for a single moment."

Laughing, Meagan stepped into his embrace. "We shall see," she teased, her blue eyes lit up with mischief. "On occasion, I can be quite tiresome."

Edward grinned as an echo of his old life flashed before his eyes. "Is that a threat?"

His wife shrugged. "A challenge, maybe. Will ye accept it? Or walk away?"

Kissing her fiercely, Edward then stood back, looking down into her beautiful face. "I will stay for as long as ye want me."

A grin came to her lips. "Would forever suit ye, dear husband?"

Smiling, Edward nodded. "Very much so, dear wife."

Epilogue

Late Autumn 1807

After almost a year of hard work, Huntington House and its surrounding cottages and farms shone in new splendour. It was a beautiful sight to behold, and Meagan could barely tear her eyes from the festive celebration held in the gardens.

Although of various social standing, people mingled freely, their smiling faces proof that love and friendship knew no bounds.

Over in the shade by the small cluster of trees that still marked the new beginning of their little family, Meagan spotted a group of tenant wives, their new babies on their arms, chatting animatedly with Derek's sister Kara as well as friends of his and his wife's. Beth Turner, Lady Elton, as well as Elsbeth Lancaster, Lady Elmridge, both new mothers themselves, had arrived with their husbands a few days before. It was a truly happy occasion where family and friends met and mingled…no matter their station.

Catching Kara's eye, Meagan smiled at her, watching as the young woman handed a piece of fruit to her little daughter. Barely a year old, little Claire was already walking like one born to it, considering crawling beneath her. No matter how often she fell, she would always push herself back up onto her chubby little legs and continue.

Catching a glimpse of her own children, Meagan turned toward them, watching them as they chased each other around the tables filled with Bessy's delicious food. Unable to chide them for their rambunctious behaviour, she smiled, brushing a hand over her flat stomach, wondering how best to share the happy news with her husband.

As though her thoughts had called him, Edward appeared beside her, gently pulling her hand into his while his other rested on his cane, his eyes aglow with happiness. "'Tis a beautiful day, isn't it?"

Although Edward often walked with a cane, he knew he no longer needed it to keep his balance. Ever since that day when he had rushed to save his daughter, he had come to realise how capable he still was. Although he had to adapt, there was nothing he could not do. To this day, he thought it a challenge to reclaim every single part of his life, finding new ways of doing old things. He rode and worked around the house as always. He still danced with her. And he climbed trees with his son and daughter.

Nothing could stop him.

His injured leg was a part of him, but Edward refused to let it keep him from life any longer.

Meagan had never seen him so alive. "A most beautiful day indeed."

He chuckled, glancing around. "It seems wherever ye look, babies are born. Has it always been like this? Or am I not very observant?"

Laughing, Meagan shrugged. "Babies have always been born. Only over the past year, we've all become...a family, sharing in each other's happiness. 'Tis different now." Watching her husband, Meagan noticed his eyes darkening. "Are ye all right?"

Sighing, he shook his head before looking at Erin running after Matthew and Collin. "On some days more than others, I feel the loss of not having been here when she grew up. One moment she was a baby, and the next, she's a little girl." Inhaling deeply, he smiled. "An amazing little girl."

"That she is," Meagan agreed, reaching for both her husband's hands. Then she stepped to the side toward a laurel bush, pulling him with her.

A bit of a frown came to his face as his gaze turned to her expectantly. "Is somethin' wrong?"

"Not at all." Swallowing, Meagan looked up at him, feeling her heart hammering in her chest with a new lightness. "I know there's nothin' I can do to change the past, to give ye back the years ye've lost, but I can give ye a new chance to watch your child grow from a baby into a little person."

For a moment, his brows creased further before his eyes opened wide with understanding. "Are ye...? Do ye mean to say...?" His gaze dropped to her flat stomach before returning to meet her gaze.

Meagan nodded, suddenly too overcome to speak.

For a moment, time seemed to stand still before Edward allowed his cane to clatter to the ground, swept her into his arms and spun her around in a circle, laughing with such delight that Meagan's heart felt it would burst with joy.

As everyone around them clapped and laughed, sharing in their happiness, Meagan knew that life was perfect. It had not been easy, but it had been well worth it.

THE END

Thank you for reading *Sacrificed & Reclaimed*!

In the next and for now final installment of this series, we get to meet Adelaide and Matthew again from book 4, *Betrayed & Blessed*!

When Adelaide's father loses her hand in a game of cards, she turns to an old friend for help. Before she knows what is happening, she finds herself married to a stranger by the name of MATTHEW TURNER, a young baron, who harbors a secret affection for her.

Is there a chance for a happily-ever-after after all?

Read a Sneak-peek

Destroyed & Restored
The Baron's Courageous Wife

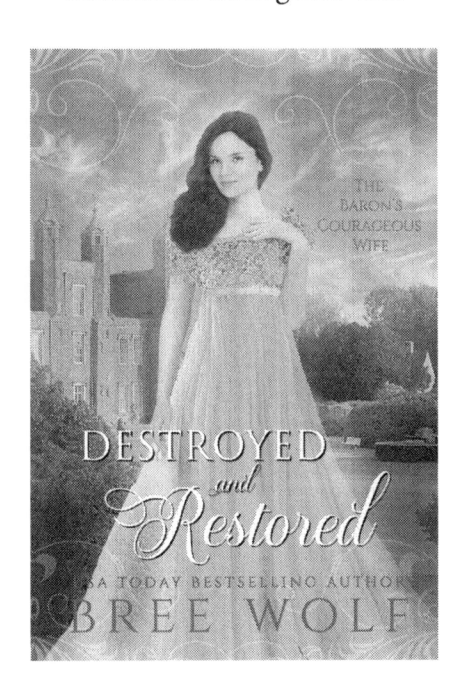

Prologue

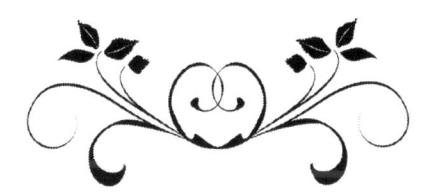

LONDON, SPRING 1807 (OR A VARIATION THEREOF)

"You deserve this!" Matthew's father sneered as he glared down at his nephew Tristan, aiming the pistol in his hands at the young man's heart. "You were never worthy!"

Matthew's own heart tightened painfully in his chest as he watched in shock. As he saw Tristan's gaze shift to his wife, tears streaming down her face. As he saw her scramble to her feet, desperate to save her husband's life. As he saw his own father for the man he truly was.

A madman.

Consumed by greed.

About to become a murderer and rip their family apart for good.

Before Matthew had formed a conscious thought, he felt himself move. He felt himself lunge forward, arms outstretched toward his father. He felt his heart thudding in his chest and his breath catch in his throat as all eyes turned to him in shock.

Then he saw his father move.

Swing around.

Toward him.

The pistol in his hands finding a new target.

PROLOGUE

And then a deafening sound shattered the peaceful stillness of the early morning air. Instantly, Matthew was thrown backwards into the wet grass of the clearing, red hot pain searing through his left shoulder.

With a groan, Matthew Turner, Baron Whitworth, shot up in bed, his heart beating through his chest as though it was trying to flee his body and seek cover elsewhere. Sweat trickled down his temples, and his breath came in ragged gasps. His eyes were wide open, and yet, they did not see the dim surroundings of his chamber. All they saw were the white clouds that had hung in the pale blue sky that morning. All he heard were his father's angry snarls. All he felt was the fresh pain drilling a hole into his heart.

His fingers travelled to his left shoulder and slipped under his shirt, finding the small scar where the bullet had broken his skin and dug itself into his body. And yet, it had been his heart that had hurt the most. So excruciating had been the pain, that for a moment Matthew had been certain the bullet had found its mark perfectly.

Closing his eyes, Matthew brushed the hair from his face, then flung back the blanket and stepped from the bed. The cool floorboards felt heavenly under his heated feet, and he welcomed the chill of the early morning air as it sent shivers over his body.

Yet another night had ended before it should have, he surmised, pulling back the curtains and staring outside at the darkened sky. His nightmares always found him sometime after midnight, dragging him back to the morning when he had finally realised the truth.

That his father had been a madman. A man willing to murder his own blood in order to steal title and fortune for himself.

And for his son.

For Matthew.

And Matthew had not seen it. In fact, he had always believed his father when the man had spoken harshly of Tristan's faults. He had always agreed that Tristan had brought shame to their family and had not deserved to hold the title passed on to him by his father. Always had Matthew berated his cousin for his inappropriate behaviour, unable to see that all Tristan's demons had been conjured by none other than his own father.

PROLOGUE

Remembering the crazed look on his father's face, Matthew closed his eyes, inhaling a deep breath. Fortunately-if that was indeed the right word! -Matthew had not died that day.

And neither had Tristan.

In the nick of time, when Matthew's father had once more advanced on his nephew after accidentally shooting his own son, Tristan's sister had arrived on the scene. Henrietta had always been an unusual woman, and as Matthew now knew, she had always protected her little brother from their uncle's destructive plans. It had been Henrietta who had stopped their uncle for good, her dagger's aim true as it always was.

If it had not been for her, Tristan would have died that day, and who knew who else would have followed him to the grave. Matthew sighed. Indeed, it was good that she had come. That she had stopped his father. That she had saved them all.

Matthew knew this to be true, and he also knew that the part of him that felt regret was the most selfish part of him there was. Still, he could not help but regret his father's death for it had robbed him of any hope for closure.

For answers.

Leaning his forehead against the cool pane of the window, Matthew closed his eyes, knowing that his mind would immediately conjure the morning in Hyde Park that had changed his life. Guilt and shame flooded him for having allowed his father to deceive-to manipulate-him so easily.

All his life, Matthew had sought his father's approval, his praise, his attention, and it had blinded him to the truth. Always had he been jealous of Tristan because all his father would concern himself with was his young nephew.

But never his son.

Never him.

Never Matthew.

Gritting his teeth, Matthew felt the strong urge to put his fist through the glass. He had been selfish and vain and foolish, and it had almost destroyed them all.

Still, Tristan had forgiven him. More than that. Tristan had not even wanted to hear of an apology when Matthew had sought him out after the shooting. He had looked him in the eyes and said that they had all been equally blind and that he was not to blame.

Matthew had been thunderstruck by his cousin's kind heart, and the guilt and shame that had taken up permanent residence in his soul had grown tenfold that day. He had vowed then that he would do whatever he could to prove himself to his family.

To prove his love.

His loyalty.

His devotion.

To prove to himself that he was not the man his father had been. To prove to himself that he was a good man. To redeem himself in his own eyes as much as in theirs. To become his own person and not live his life in his father's image.

Again, his fingers curled into a fist, and Matthew had to step away from the window to resist temptation.

As irony would have it, not long after his father's death, Matthew had inherited the title of baron through his mother's line when a distant cousin had died childless in a riding accident. The day he had received the news had been one of the darkest days of his life.

To Matthew, it was as though his father was reaching out his hands from the grave, forcing his idea of right and wrong on him. Forcing Matthew to live the life his father had been willing to kill for.

Would he ever feel at peace again? Would he ever be able to look at himself in the mirror and not feel shame and guilt? Would he ever be his own man? Or was he doomed to follow in his father's footsteps?

He would do anything to gain back even just the smallest piece of respect he used to have for himself.

Anything.

Before it was too late.

Series Overview

LOVE'S SECOND CHANCE: TALES OF LORDS & LADIES

LOVE'S SECOND CHANCE: TALES OF DAMSELS & KNIGHTS

LOVE'S SECOND CHANCE: HIGHLAND TALES

SERIES OVERVIEW

FORBIDDEN LOVE SERIES

HAPPY EVER REGENCY SERIES

THE WHICKERTONS IN LOVE

For more information visit www.breewolf.com

About Bree

USA Today bestselling and award-winning author, Bree Wolf has always been a language enthusiast (though not a grammarian!) and is rarely found without a book in her hand or her fingers glued to a keyboard. Trying to find her way, she has taught English as a second language, traveled abroad and worked at a translation agency as well as a law firm in Ireland. She also spent loooong years obtaining a BA in English and Education and an MA in Specialized Translation while wishing she could simply be a writer. Although there is nothing simple about being a writer, her dreams have finally come true.

"A big thanks to my fairy godmother!"

Currently, Bree has found her new home in the historical romance genre, writing Regency novels and novellas. Enjoying the mix of fact and fiction, she occasionally feels like a puppet master (or mistress? Although that sounds weird!), forcing her characters into ever-new situations that will put their strength, their beliefs, their love to the test, hoping that in the end they will triumph and get the happily-ever-after we are all looking for.

If you're an avid reader, sign up for Bree's newsletter on **www.breewolf.com** as she has the tendency to simply give books away. Find out about freebies, giveaways as well as occasional advance reader copies and read before the book is even on the shelves!

Connect with Bree and stay up-to-date on new releases:

- facebook.com/breewolf.novels
- twitter.com/breewolf_author
- instagram.com/breewolf_author
- bookbub.com/authors/bree-wolf
- amazon.com/Bree-Wolf/e/B00FJX27Z4

Printed by Amazon Italia Logistica S.r.l.
Torrazza Piemonte (TO), Italy